A PRINCESS PRAYS

Father Jozsef did not make a move to accompany her as Attila ran across the garden and up the steps into the Chapel.

As she expected there were flowers on the altar and in every window and there was the fragrance of incense.

Also there was something Attila had never found in any other Church.

It was an atmosphere of holiness, which at the same time seemed to pulsate with a life force.

It could only have come from God Himself.

Attila sank down on her knees in front of the altar and although Father Jozsef was not with her she knew he was blessing her.

She prayed fervently,

'Please God restore my Papa to good health. He is so needed here in Valdina and there is no one to take his place.'

She paused and bowed her head low as if she was pleading with God to hear her prayer.

'Let me find love. The true love Papa and Mama had for each other which they always believed came from You. I have no wish to be married except to a man who loves me as a woman not as a Princess and I will love him for himself and for no other reason.'

Her voice dropped as she begged,

'Help me, God, *please help me*, because I cannot manage my life without You.'

THE BARBARA CARTLAND PINK COLLECTION

Titles in this series

1. The Cross Of Love
2. Love In The Highlands
3. Love Finds The Way
4. The Castle Of Love
5. Love Is Triumphant
6. Stars In The Sky
7. The Ship Of Love
8. A Dangerous Disguise
9. Love Became Theirs
10. Love Drives In
11. Sailing To Love
12. The Star Of Love
13. Music Is The Soul Of Love
14. Love In The East
15. Theirs To Eternity
16. A Paradise On Earth
17. Love Wins In Berlin
18. In Search Of Love
19. Love Rescues Rosanna
20. A Heart In Heaven
21. The House Of Happiness
22. Royalty Defeated By Love
23. The White Witch
24. They Sought Love
25. Love Is The Reason For Living
26. They Found Their Way To Heaven
27. Learning To Love
28. Journey To Happiness
29. A Kiss In The Desert
30. The Heart Of Love
31. The Richness Of Love
32. For Ever And Ever
33. An Unexpected Love
34. Saved By An Angel
35. Touching The Stars
36. Seeking Love
37. Journey To Love
38. The Importance Of Love
39. Love By The Lake
40. A Dream Come True
41. The King Without A Heart
42. The Waters Of Love
43. Danger To The Duke
44. A Perfect Way To Heaven
45. Follow Your Heart
46. In Hiding
47. Rivals For Love
48. A Kiss From The Heart
49. Lovers In London
50. This Way To Heaven
51. A Princess Prays

A PRINCESS PRAYS

BARBARA CARTLAND

Barbaracartland.com Ltd

First published on the internet in December 2008
by Barbaracartland.com

ISBN 978-1-905155-99-6

The characters and situations in this book are entirely imaginary and bear no relation to any real person or actual happening.

Printed and bound in Great Britain by Cle-Print Ltd.
of St Ives, Cambridgeshire.

THE BARBARA CARTLAND PINK COLLECTION

Barbara Cartland was the most prolific bestselling author in the history of the world. She was frequently in the Guinness Book of Records for writing more books in a year than any other living author. In fact her most amazing literary feat was when her publishers asked for more Barbara Cartland romances, she doubled her output from 10 books a year to over 20 books a year, when she was 77.

She went on writing continuously at this rate for 20 years and wrote her last book at the age of 97, thus completing 400 books between the ages of 77 and 97.

Her publishers finally could not keep up with this phenomenal output, so at her death she left 160 unpublished manuscripts, something again that no other author has ever achieved.

Now the exciting news is that these 160 original unpublished Barbara Cartland books are already being published and by Barbaracartland.com exclusively on the internet, as the international web is the best possible way of reaching so many Barbara Cartland readers around the world.

The 160 books are published monthly and will be numbered in sequence.

The series is called the Pink Collection as a tribute to Barbara Cartland whose favourite colour was pink and it became very much her trademark over the years.

The Barbara Cartland Pink Collection is published only on the internet. Log on to www.barbaracartland.com to find out how you can purchase the books monthly as they are published, and take out a subscription that will ensure that all subsequent editions are delivered to you by mail order to your home.

NEW

Barbaracartland.com is proud to announce the publication of ten new Audio Books for the first time as CDs. They are favourite Barbara Cartland stories read by well-known actors and actresses and each story extends to 4 or 5 CDs. The Audio Books are as follows:

The Patient Bridegroom	The Passion and the Flower
A Challenge of Hearts	Little White Doves of Love
A Train to Love	The Prince and the Pekinese
The Unbroken Dream	A King in Love
The Cruel Count	A Sign of Love

More Audio Books will be published in the future and the above titles can be purchased by logging on to the website www.barbaracartland.com or please write to the address below.

If you do not have access to a computer, you can write for information about the Barbara Cartland Pink Collection and the Barbara Cartland Audio Books to the following address:

Barbara Cartland.com Ltd., Camfield Place,
Hatfield, Hertfordshire AL9 6JE, United Kingdom.

Telephone: +44 (0)1707 642629
Fax: +44 (0)1707 663041

THE LATE DAME BARBARA CARTLAND

Barbara Cartland who sadly died in May 2000 at the age of nearly 99 was the world's most famous romantic novelist who wrote 723 books in her lifetime with worldwide sales of over 1 billion copies and her books were translated into 36 different languages.

As well as romantic novels, she wrote historical biographies, 6 autobiographies, theatrical plays, books of advice on life, love, vitamins and cookery. She also found time to be a political speaker and television and radio personality.

She wrote her first book at the age of 21 and this was called *Jigsaw*. It became an immediate bestseller and sold 100,000 copies in hardback and was translated into 6 different languages. She wrote continuously throughout her life, writing bestsellers for an astonishing 76 years. Her books have always been immensely popular in the United States, where in 1976 her current books were at numbers 1 & 2 in the B. Dalton bestsellers list, a feat never achieved before or since by any author.

Barbara Cartland became a legend in her own lifetime and will be best remembered for her wonderful romantic novels, so loved by her millions of readers throughout the world.

Her books will always be treasured for their moral message, her pure and innocent heroines, her good looking and dashing heroes and above all her belief that the power of love is more important than anything else in everyone's life.

"It is my firm belief that anyone who prays fervently and sincerely from the heart and soul will always be listened to."

Barbara Cartland

CHAPTER ONE
1798

Princess Attila walked into the Palace and up the stairs as she was heading for her father's bedroom.

The King had not been at all well for several weeks and she knew he would be very pleased with the first wild strawberries she had found.

Every day she tried to find something different to take him.

When he could not walk into his garden which he enjoyed – "the garden," she said, "had to come to him."

The Palace was very ancient as it had been in the possession of the Kings of Valdina for over three hundred years.

A few modern improvements had been made when Attila's mother was alive, but they had found it easier to leave things as they were.

As far as her father was concerned he was always very comfortable.

Sadly, his new wife, Attila's stepmother, had very different ideas. As Queen Margit she was quite determined to make an impression not only to the people of Valdina, but also on their neighbours.

The Royal Family of Hungary, however, were not very interested in the smaller countries on their borders and Queen Margit found this infuriating as she always wished to move in grand Royal circles.

Princess Attila was content to ride the magnificent horses her father had brought from Hungary.

She was not in the least concerned whether she was invited to balls and social functions at the Palace.

As she now walked towards her father's suite she was thinking.

It would be a mistake, as he was not feeling well, if her stepmother continued to entertain as many people as she had in the last few months.

She gave luncheons, dinner parties and receptions almost every day.

If a visitor of any importance appeared in Valdina she insisted on being notified and then she would invite everyone within driving distance to come to the Palace.

The majority of the Queen's friends boasted titles of Social importance and were therefore usually middle-aged or ancient.

Attila was always polite to them and yet she often mused it would be more amusing if some young people of her own age were invited.

She was eighteen and having been an only child she had found her life lonely at times.

As soon as her father had married again the new Queen was extremely particular who was entertained at the Palace.

"I consider those middle class people that you told me are so interesting are of no Social importance," she said severely to Attila, "thus I have no intention of entertaining them!"

"But the young men of their family are outstanding athletes," the Princess protested. "They have not only won all the races held in the country this year, but have a superb reputation even in Hungary."

"I still have no intention of them sitting round my dining room table," the Queen had retorted sharply.

Attila wanted to argue the issue out with her father, but he was not well and she knew it might worry him.

She therefore had to be content with watching the young men whom she admired from the Royal Box and she thought they were rather disappointed at not being asked to the Palace.

So were the athletes who came to the country from Moravia and Silesia, both countries on their borders.

Because Valdina was not very large her mother had always made a point of being friendly to their neighbours. And gave them invitations whenever possible.

Attila had now arrived at her father's bedroom door and was just about to knock when she realised the door was slightly ajar.

She could hear her stepmother speaking inside and for a moment Attila hesitated.

She wondered if she should wait till her father was alone before she joined him.

But then she heard her stepmother saying,

"The sooner Attila is married off the better. I have invited Prince Otto of Dedregen to dinner next week."

Attila stiffened as she heard her father reply slowly,

"I cannot remember him at all. But I thought I had heard something about him which was not particularly to his advantage."

Queen Margit gave an affected little laugh.

"I think you must have been reading some of the salacious news they write in the newspapers, or listening to one of your more tiresome courtiers who will always have something unpleasant to say about anyone of importance."

"I am certain I have heard something about Prince Otto," the King murmured.

Attila knew exactly what her father was trying to remember.

There had been a scandal last year.

It had been whispered amongst the Royal families that Prince Otto had seduced a young woman. She lived in an adjacent country and she was, Attila heard, attempting to sue him for refusing to marry her.

It was said she had many letters in her possession from the Prince which were very incriminating.

For weeks there had been a great deal of gossip and then the woman in question was paid a very large sum to disappear and no one was at all certain where she went.

Apart from this allegation, Prince Otto was talked of as a womaniser.

Attila could remember one of her mother's friends saying she had no intention of entertaining him or allowing him to meet her daughters.

She could hardly believe it that her stepmother was actually encouraging him on her behalf.

As if the King was thinking the same he asked,

"Why would you think Prince Otto is interested in Attila? I cannot remember him coming here?"

"Apparently he was not invited," the Queen replied sharply. "I met him the other night when I dined with the Grand Duke. His Royal Highness told me that he was longing to meet Attila as he had heard so much of her beauty and her charm."

She paused then continued impressively,

"As he will eventually reign in Dedregen when his father dies, I was sensible enough to invite him here. After all it will be an excellent marriage for Attila."

"There is no hurry," replied the King firmly. "As I have no son I want my people, when I die, to accept her as the Queen."

There was a pause and then Queen Margit said,

"You are not going to die, dearest Sigismund, for many, many years. So I think Attila would be far happier married than having to cope with all the difficulties and problems which you find so tiring.

"But you know, my dearest, I will help you in every way I can. You must tell the Prime Minister and members of the Cabinet to consult me, which they will not do at the moment."

Attila drew in her breath as she knew now exactly what her stepmother was trying to do.

Her father, when they had been alone, had told her that as he had no son, she would have to take his place.

It would not be unusual for Valdina to be ruled by a Queen.

Fifty years ago there had been a very distinguished female ancestor, who had not only reigned superbly over the country but had fought endless battles against Moravia and won.

Attila understood exactly what her father wanted from her.

She had recognised why she had been given such an extensive education, which was certainly unusual where women were concerned.

Her father and mother had insisted on Attila being taught by tutors in all the main subjects and she had in fact received the education of a boy by the time she had left the schoolroom.

Her father had married again because he was lonely and he missed her mother almost unbearably.

Attila had realised from the very moment that her stepmother had arrived at the Palace that she was jealous of her.

Queen Margit was, in reality, a pushy woman who wanted to lord it over everyone she met – most especially over her stepdaughter.

Attila had rather suspected what she really wanted and that was to become the Ruler of Valdina if the King, who was far older than she was, should die.

She was therefore contriving to be rid of Attila who knew that if she married a reigning Prince there would be no question of her reigning over Valdina.

She had by now been living with her stepmother for more than three years and realised that she was tenacious and determined in every particular to get her own way.

Attila also recognised that if Prince Otto proposed, the Queen would do everything in her power to force her into accepting him.

It did not surprise her at all that her father did not know as she did all the unsavoury things about Prince Otto.

The King was never interested in gossip and when the Palace women started whispering amongst themselves, he always sat in his own room as he had no wish to be bored by them.

It would have been impossible for her not to have heard that Prince Otto had a very unpleasant character.

There was also secret gossip about him which was considered too improper for her young ears.

'What am I to do?' Attila asked herself frantically.

Then she heard the Queen say,

"I am going to leave you now, dearest Sigismund, because you must rest. Do not worry because I can assure you I have Attila's future very much at heart. Dedregen is a most attractive country and rather larger than ours."

She must have risen to her feet as she was speaking, for now Attila could hear her footsteps on the stone floor.

Softly so that her stepmother would not see her, she opened another door and slipped into a small side room as her stepmother passed and continued on down the passage.

She waited until she was out of sight and then she went into her father's room.

She walked to the bed, bent down and kissed him.

"How are you feeling, Papa?" she asked him. "I do hope you are well enough to eat these wild strawberries I have brought for you. I know you like them better than the ones which grow in the garden."

"Strawberries!" exclaimed the King. "That means summer is here and we must enjoy every minute of it."

"I think we deserve it after that very hard winter," Attila agreed.

She sat down beside the bed.

"I have a distinct feeling, Papa," she began softly, "that Stepmama has been talking to you about my being married. I have no wish to marry anyone and I am very happy here with you."

"Which is just where I want you to be, my darling. At the same time your stepmother is insistent that you look round at the eligible young men and she seems to have one particularly in mind – "

"I think that you must be referring to Prince Otto of Dredregen and I can tell you now, dear Papa, he has a very unpleasant reputation. I know Mama would not approve of him coming here to the Palace, let alone wishing to marry me!"

She spoke so vehemently that the King reached out and patted her hand.

"Now, now, my dearest. We know nothing at all

about this young man. He may be very desirable and your stepmother feels quite rightly that you should have a home of your own."

"I cannot see anything right about it," she asserted "and there is no real reason for me to hurry into marriage."

"No, no of course not," agreed the King. "At the same time I married your darling mother the day before her eighteenth birthday. It was undoubtedly the best and most wonderful thing that could possibly have ever happened to me."

There was anguish in her father's voice, which was what Attila always heard when he spoke about her mother.

"Mama knew you were so happy, because she told me you both fell in love the moment you met one another."

The King nodded.

"That is so very true. When I first saw your mother I thought I was meeting an angel from Heaven and that is exactly what she was when she married me."

"Mama told me how handsome and charming you were. So you will understand, Papa, that I want to fall in love in the same way and not be pushed off on some Prince who in Stepmama's eyes is of great dynastic importance."

There was silence for a moment then the King said,

"I have not told you, Attila, because I did not want to upset you, but the doctors who examined me two days ago are very worried about my condition."

"Oh no, Papa! What is wrong? I thought you were just tired."

"If I am to be truthful," he replied, "I have to face the fact that I will not live for very long. I have a disease, my dearest, for which there is no known cure. Although I may live for several years, it will not be longer than that."

"*Papa*!"

Atilla gave a loud cry of horror as she bent forward to put her arms round her father's neck.

"Oh, Papa, how could this happen to you?"

"I am afraid it happens to a large number of people and the doctors are not as clever as they pretend to be."

"But surely there must be somewhere we can go? Perhaps Germany or Spain?"

The King shook his head.

"The doctors say it would be quite useless and the journey would make me worse."

There were tears in Attila's eyes as she pleaded,

"I cannot lose you too, Papa. When I lost Mama I thought it was the end of the world, but if I lose you too – "

Her voice broke and she could not say any more.

The King pulled her close to him.

"I know what you are feeling, my precious, and I am only so grateful that your mother is not here, because it would upset her so much."

Attila was fighting hard against tears and could not speak as her father continued,

"I always wanted you to reign in my place when I died, but I think you will be too young. Therefore perhaps it would be for the best, as your stepmother suggests, if you make a life for yourself somewhere else."

He gave a deep sigh.

"Being a Ruler brings a great number of problems and difficulties with it, which I feel would be too much for a woman. Therefore, my darling daughter, please consider what your stepmother has proposed."

As the King finished speaking, he closed his eyes.

Although he did not say so, Attila was aware he did not wish to discuss the matter further.

She kissed her father before walking to the window wiping away her tears.

She stood staring at the garden bathed in sunshine.

With the spring flowers in bloom and the trees in blossom it looked very lovely.

'How is it possible,' Attila asked herself, 'with so much loveliness around me that there should be this pain and horror of what my dear Papa had just told me?'

How could she let him go?

Her whole life was centred on him, even though life had never been the same since her mother died.

She stood at the window for some minutes and then she became aware that her father had fallen asleep.

Very softly she tip-toed from the room, leaving the strawberries she had brought him beside his bed.

Outside Attila saw one of the *aides-de-camp*.

He was a gentleman she had never much cared for, as she believed he sucked up to her stepmother, flattering her and paying her fulsome compliments.

Attila was certain in her heart that he did not really mean them.

He had observed Attila emerging from the King's bedroom and now bowing subserviently, he said,

"I was looking for Your Royal Highness."

"Why?"

"Her Majesty the Queen has asked me to find you as she wishes you to join her in the blue drawing room."

Attila felt no desire to talk with her stepmother and yet she knew it would be rude if she refused to do what the *aide-de-camp* asked.

She therefore slowly descended the stairs.

The blue drawing room was only used by the Royal

family when they were not entertaining. The many grand State rooms in the middle of the Palace were too large and overpowering to be comfortable when they were alone.

Queen Margit was sitting at her writing table near the window and when Attila entered the room, she looked up and rose to her feet.

"Oh, there you are, Attila. They have been a long time in finding you. Where have you been?"

"I was with Papa."

She saw her stepmother purse her lips together as if she was annoyed.

Then she sat down on the sofa.

"I want to talk to you."

"What about?" enquired Attila. "I was just going to the stables."

"The horses can wait. I want to talk to you about yourself."

Attila thought she knew what was coming.

"I think that is a very dull subject! I want to talk about Papa. I am extremely upset at learning that he is not well."

To her surprise her stepmother gave what sounded like a laugh, a very artificial one at that.

"You must not believe all your father tells you. He has it in his head that he will not get better. The doctors tell me it is just part of his imagination. After all he is still a young man and I think it extremely unlikely that there is anything seriously wrong with him."

Attila stared at her stepmother in astonishment.

After what her father had told her it was impossible to believe that she was telling the truth.

"What I am now determined is that as your father is a little distressed at the moment, he will not be made worse by anyone upsetting him."

She paused a moment before continuing,

"If there is any likelihood of him not getting better, I am sure he would be most worried about your future. To be quite frank, Attila, I think it would be best for you to marry and have a family of your own."

There was silence for a moment then Attila said,

"If Papa is seriously ill as he believes, he would, I know, want me to rule over Valdina as Queen Dorottya did so successfully."

The Queen gave the scornful laugh.

"You really think that you could emulate and be as successful as Queen Dorottya? My dear child you flatter yourself. Your great-great-grandmother was an exception to every rule. It is a great mistake, I assure you, for women to try to rule a country and they are seldom successful."

There was a fraught silence.

Then Attila, who had been so well educated, could not resist responding,

"What about Queen Elizabeth of England? Surely no one could say that she was not the equal if not superior to the Kings who preceded and succeeded her."

She knew as she spoke that her stepmother had not even heard of Queen Elizabeth, or if she had, knew very little about her.

"We are not concerned in any way," Queen Margit retorted sharply, "with what happens in England or for that matter in any other country."

She pursed her lips again.

"It is Valdina we are talking about and if there is to be a woman on the throne, she must be experienced enough to be capable of ruling this beloved country of ours as well as your father has done."

There was a sudden shining light in her eyes.

It told Attila all too clearly that her stepmother now intended to take her father's place.

She could almost imagine her informing the Prime Minister and all those concerned that she would make the perfect Queen for the country and that a young girl with no experience of the world would be a disaster.

Queen Margit broke the silence.

"I have now arranged," she said firmly, "for Prince Otto of Dedregen to come here next week. He is anxious to meet you and I really think, dear child, you must not be surprised if he proposes marriage."

She looked at Attila imperiously.

"It is an alliance which I am convinced would make your father very happy and I feel certain that is what you want him to be."

She spoke in a most insistent manner, almost Attila thought as if she was trying to hypnotise her into doing as she wanted.

Slowly and with a dignity that betrayed her Royal blood, Attila rose to her feet.

"I think, Stepmama, it is always a big mistake to anticipate what people will do or not do, especially when it concerns anything as serious as marriage."

Her voice became very firm and determined.

"The one thing I can assure you is that I have no intention of marrying anyone I do not love and who does not love me for myself and not for my position in life."

The Queen would have interrupted but she finished,

"That is all I have to say on this matter and I do not wish to discuss it again."

She walked towards the door and had left the room before the Queen could answer her.

Outside in the hall Attila ran out of the front door and into the garden.

She was running away from what was frightening and disturbing her.

Her one idea at the moment was to be alone and she knew she must think clearly and decide what to do.

The sunshine was warm and the garden was ablaze with spring flowers, but Attila could think only of what her father had told her.

The future ahead now seemed to be covered by a growing darkness.

'What can I do? What can I do,' she asked herself.

She walked on past the fountains and the water lily pond. There was a profusion of almond trees in blossom everywhere and she reached the shrubbery.

The twisting path under the trees made her slow her pace.

Now she began to feel she could breathe again.

She walked on until she came to an opening in the trees that looked down on a little valley.

At the end, its roof just peeping above the branches, was a little Chapel.

Attila knew it so well.

It was a very ancient Chapel and had been built by one of her ancestors, who had retired there after she was widowed and never entered the Palace again.

Now the Chapel and the adjoining room were used by Father Jozsef.

He was a very old Priest whom she had known and loved ever since she was a small child and he had prepared her for Confirmation.

Because she had been busy with her father and with her tutors, she had not seen Father Jozsef for some time.

She thought now he was the one person who would understand the predicament she was in.

There was a twisting path beneath the trees leading down to the valley and when she reached the Chapel she saw that the flowers were in bloom all around it.

She knew that they had always been the delight of Father Jozsef and he tended to them as if they were his children.

She went first into the Chapel, which was small but exquisite with its old carvings and beautiful stained-glass windows.

Father Jozsef was not present, but when she went round the back of the Chapel she found him, as she might have expected, weeding his garden.

The Father was wearing an ancient cassock and his white hair was blowing a little in the breeze.

Although he was nearly at the age of eighty he still remained a handsome and prepossessing figure.

Attila always believed it was his personality rather than his looks that captivated all who met him.

She stood watching him for a few moments before he turned round, as if he instinctively sensed her presence.

He gave a cry of delight, threw down his trowel and walked towards her holding out his hands.

"My child, my beloved Princess, how glad I am to see you!" he exclaimed.

"And I to see you. You must forgive me, Father Jozsef, if I have neglected you lately, but Papa is not well and I spend every moment I can with him."

"I had heard your father was in ill health and I have been praying for him as I know you would have expected me to do."

"He needs your prayers badly and I, Father, need your help."

He smiled at her.

"Let us sit down," he suggested.

They walked towards a wooden seat on one side of his garden.

They sat down and Father Jozsef enquired,

"Tell me what is worrying you. You know, if it is at all possible with God's help, I will solve your problem for you."

Attila smiled.

"I knew you would say that to me, Father, and as I am worried, very, very worried, I have come to you as I have always done ever since I could toddle."

"I know and a very pretty little toddler you were. As you know, Attila, I have loved you as if you were my own ever since you were born."

Attila put out her hand and slipped it into his.

"Help me," she pleaded, "because I not only need it badly, but I am so very frightened."

"I am listening, my child."

Attila told him what she had overheard outside her father's door and what the King had said to her.

Next she repeated her stepmother's words and saw his lips tighten.

"I have just left my Stepmama," she finished, "and instinctively without really thinking about it I came straight to you."

"It was God who directed you knowing it was the most sensible thing you could do, my child."

"I am so so frightened, Father. Frightened that she will force Papa to agree to my marriage and if he begs me to do it for his sake, it will be very hard for me to refuse."

Father Jozsef nodded as if he agreed this was likely to happen.

Then he said firmly,

"There is one thing I am completely sure about and it is that under no circumstances must you marry His Royal Highness Prince Otto."

"You have heard about him?" asked Attila.

"A great deal and I can only tell you now that it is impossible for you, pure innocent and unspoilt as you are, to marry such a man."

"Then what can I do? Stepmama wishes to be rid of me and she will somehow contrive, just as she has done before, to make Papa agree."

She paused for a moment.

"And I can tell you about enumerable times when against his better inclination, dear Papa has agreed simply because it is easier than opposing her."

Father Jozsef did not speak and Attila carried on,

"I am convinced in my own mind that she wants to rule when Papa dies as if she was Queen Dorottya."

"It would not surprise me," remarked Father Jozsef.

"If she really cared for others I would not mind, but she is not in any way interested in anyone but herself even though she pretends to be."

She sighed.

"When the servants are ill she is only angry because it is inconvenient. If she hears of any trouble in the City or anywhere else in Valdina, she will not listen."

She made a gesture of helplessness with her hands.

"They have heard her say when people have asked for her help, 'if they have got themselves into a mess they had better find how to get out of it. It is not *my* business'."

"I don't think," reflected Father Jozsef, "that the Government or the people of Valdina would allow Queen

Margit to take the throne, but of course if you were married and lived elsewhere, there would in fact be no one else who had any right to it."

Attila sighed again.

"If only I had a brother or I had been born a boy".

Father Jozsef smiled.

"I think you will find that there are a great number of men who are pleased you are a woman, but at the same time is there no man in your life for whom you have any affection?"

"Of course not. I never meet any young men. My Stepmama will only entertain those who are distinguished and important. This means they are usually as old at Papa and even Prince Otto whom I believe is under thirty would never be invited to the Palace unless he was the heir to a throne."

"It was very different when your dear mother was alive. Then she received everyone and the people loved her because they knew she loved them."

"I have missed her more than I can ever say," Attila sighed, "and I miss her so much now. Oh, Father Jozsef, *you* are the only person who can help me."

Father Jozsef rose to his feet.

"I am going to pray that I shall give my beloved little Princess the right advice. Wait for me here and listen to the song of the birds and watch the butterflies. I will not be long."

He turned as he spoke and walked away and Attila knew he would go into the Chapel to kneel in front of the altar and wait for God to give him his instructions.

It was what he had done ever since she had known him as a child.

She had asked him once when she was very small,

"Does God talk to you, Father? Can you hear Him when He is so high up in Heaven?"

"God always speaks to us," Father Jozsef had told her, "through our souls and our brains."

"How does He do that?" Attila had asked.

"You will learn when you are older, my child, that when you close your eyes and ask God to help you, you need to wait for a few minutes. Then suddenly the answer is there in your mind. It is just as if you had read it in a book or heard someone say it to you."

At the time, Attila, who had only been five years old, clasped her hands together.

"I will listen very carefully," she enthused. "I will concentrate and hear the answer in my forehead."

"That is right, but you must not be too disappointed if your answer does not arrive immediately. God always knows what is best for you and also when it is best for you to have it."

Looking back over the years Attila could remember praying in the little Chapel and she also prayed beside her bed before she climbed into it. She prayed at night when she woke up and it was dark.

Now she thought about it there always seemed to be an answer sooner rather than later to whichever question she had posed.

She looked up at the sky.

'*Please* God give me an answer now,' she prayed.

Then as she glanced at the Chapel she saw Father Jozsef coming towards her.

CHAPTER TWO

Father Jozsef sat down beside Attila on the wooden seat and for a moment he did not speak and Attila looked at him enquiringly.

Then he said,

"I have a suggestion to make to you, which may at first seem rather strange, but it is one I want you to hear."

"Then of course I am listening, Father."

"You have told me your father is ill," Father Jozsef began, "but he is still a young man. I cannot believe it is impossible for him to be cured, and as you well know he is needed desperately here in Valdina."

"I am certain it would be just terrible without him," Attila murmured.

She was thinking again of her stepmother and how she would try to force herself upon the throne.

"What I am suggesting," Father Jozsef continued, "is that you and I should go on a pilgrimage."

Attila looked at him wide-eyed.

"*A pilgrimage*!" she exclaimed.

"You have heard me talk of St. Janos?"

"Yes, of course, he is the Saint whose shrine is on the top of one of the mountains where our country borders with Hungary."

"The Hungarians worship him as their own Saint," Father Jozsef told her, "but he is also ours."

"And you want me to go on a pilgrimage to him?"

She could hardly believe that was what he meant.

He nodded.

"I will come with you and we will ask St. Janos not only if it is God's will to save your father's life, but also to solve your own problem."

He smiled before he added,

"You do know that St. Janos is really the God of Love?"

Attila knew this only too well as Father Jozsef had told her the story first when she was very small and he had repeated it over the years.

She thought now she knew it word for word.

St. Janos at one time had been the Ruling Prince of a country which did not now exist and he was a good and kind Ruler.

At the same time he had a great number of enemies he needed to keep at bay.

As he grew older he wanted to marry and he looked at the countries surrounding him for a beautiful Princess.

However, those he met did not impress him, nor did he fall in love.

Then one day he was riding beside the river and as he sat down by the water he saw the most beautiful girl he had ever imagined.

He spoke briefly to her and the moment they looked into the other's eyes they both knew they belonged to each other.

It was something that they must have done in many lives before.

It was love at first sight and the Prince then became determined she should be his wife.

It was, however, not an easy decision, because the girl he had met was of quite humble origin.

Her parents were cultured people, but their blood was certainly not blue as was to be expected of the wife of a reigning Prince.

The Prince was still determined to marry her and while he was arguing with his Ministers and relations, one of them approached the girl he loved.

He told her she would ruin the Prince's life and his career if he married her.

She loved him as passionately as he loved her and she believed that he was the man she had been waiting and praying for.

Therefore she felt to lose him would be so painful that she could not go on living.

She wrote to him to say that she was not worthy of him and rather than upset his life she would return to God from where she had come and pray for his happiness.

When the Prince received her message, he became distraught at what she had written.

He rushed to her father's house across the river to find her, but he was too late.

She had climbed to the very top of a high mountain and there she had prayed and prayed for many hours before she threw herself into the river far below.

When they found her body on the jagged rocks, she still looked very lovely and ethereal.

Her eyes were firmly closed as if she had been in prayer and yet there was a faint smile on her lips because she had been thinking of the man she loved.

She had sacrificed herself for him.

Now the Prince had no wish to live his life without her, he left the Palace, surrendering the throne to a relative.

Next he built a small Shrine to his beloved at the top of the mountain from which she had thrown herself.

He stayed there in a small bare room attached to the Shrine for the rest of his life.

His people begged him to return but each time he refused, telling them that if they came to him with their problems he would do his best to solve them.

He lived to a great old age and many miracles were attributed to him.

Finally he was canonized by the Church of Rome.

The Shrine remained and many pious pilgrims from Valdina, Hungary and nearby countries like Moravia and Silesia visited it in the summer months.

In the winter it was quite impossible to get through the snow and the people said that no man could survive in such cold unless he himself was a God.

In fact St. Janos lived, it was believed, until he was over eighty, but those who visited the Shrine felt his spirit was still there.

When they prayed, they claimed they always found the answer to their problems.

Attila now thought that only St. Janos could save her father from the disease for which no doctor had a cure.

Perhaps as well he would give her an answer to her need for love.

Father Jozsef was watching her face.

He saw that her eyes were shining as she asked,

"Can we really go to the Shrine? Would it not be too far for you?"

"Nothing is ever too far if it is of real importance. I know of one thing, my child, that only God can help us and only St. Janos will tell us how."

"Then let us go," cried Attila. "If he will save Papa nothing could be too far. And perhaps as you say St. Janos will tell me now to find the real love I wish for."

"Which we all want," Father Jozsef added quietly, "and that, my child, is what you must have."

She stayed with him for a long time while he made plans.

Of one thing Attila was certain, that her stepmother would try to prevent her from leaving.

"What I must now do," she said, "is to tell Papa at the last moment and make him promise to pray, as we shall be praying, until we reach St. Janos."

He smiled before he added,

"I think it unlikely that anything evil will disturb us in any way."

Attila knew how well respected he was by everyone in Valdina and they were very proud of him because he had been with them for so long.

If a peasant couple or for that matter anyone were to be married at the Cathedral, they would inevitably seek a blessing from Father Jozsef.

Attila often thought because the people of Valdina believed in him so sincerely, it was on the whole a very happy nation.

"How soon shall we go, Father?"

"I have to get ready my travelling carriage which I have not used for so long," replied Father Jozsef. "And of course find two fine horses to pull it."

Attila made a gesture with her hands.

"Our stables are at your disposal as always."

Father Jozsef smiled.

In the days when he rode a great deal the King had

always mounted him and any of the horses in the Royal stables were at his beck and call.

He had been, when he was a young man, a very experienced horseman and Attila knew that he still rode if someone was dying and required his blessing.

"You are quite certain," she entreated, "that you do not think it will be too much for you? It is a long way, Father, and I could not bear you to be ill or suffer because you are helping me."

"I know it is God's will that I should take you to the Shrine of St. Janos," stated Father Jozsef vigorously.

The way he spoke told Attila that he did not wish to discuss the matter any further.

She therefore said,

"Thank you. Thank you, Father. I knew you would not fail me and if our prayers can make Papa better that will be a miracle all on its own."

"I feel sure that he will recover, my child, but of course it is in the hands of God."

"Then when shall we go?"

"In three day's time and with the exception of your father, who we will talk to the night before we leave, no one must have the slightest idea of where we are going."

Attila realised he was thinking of her stepmother as well as the Prime Minister and the Members of the Council who might say the mission was dangerous.

They would certainly want her to be accompanied by soldiers.

As if Father Jozsef read her thoughts, he said,

"Pilgrims go humbly and we have no wish to draw attention to ourselves by appearing to be of any particular significance."

Attila smiled.

"I will just have to look like one of your pupils, which is exactly what I am. So thank you, Father. Thank you more than I can possibly say."

She gave a little sigh.

"I suppose I must be going back. May I go into the Chapel?"

"Yes, of course, you may."

Father Jozsef did not make a move to accompany her as Attila ran across the garden and up the steps into the Chapel.

As she expected there were flowers on the altar and in every window and there was the fragrance of incense.

Also there was something Attila had never found in any other Church.

It was an atmosphere of holiness, which at the same time seemed to pulsate with a life force.

It could only have come from God Himself.

Attila sank down on her knees in front of the altar and although Father Jozsef was not with her she knew he was blessing her.

She prayed fervently,

'Please God restore my Papa to good health. He is so needed here in Valdina and there is no one to take his place.'

She paused and bowed her head low as if she was pleading with God to hear her prayer.

'Let me find love. The true love Papa and Mama had for each other which they always believed came from You. I have no wish to be married except to a man who loves me as a woman not as a Princess and I will love him for himself and for no other reason.'

Her voice dropped as she begged,

'Help me, God, *please help me*, because I cannot manage my life without You.'

It was a most sincere prayer and Attila felt it was somehow carried up into the sky.

The sunshine coming through the windows seemed to bring her a blessing and she felt sure her prayer had been heard.

Time was passing by and Attila did not want her stepmother to ask questions as to where she had been.

She left the Chapel after one final prayer.

When she went outside she saw that Father Jozsef was back working on his flowers.

She ran to him and when he saw the expression on her face, he said,

"I know my child that God has heard your prayer."

"I will come and see you tomorrow, Father."

"I think that would be a mistake. As you have not been here for some time it may seem strange that you are continuously calling on me."

Attila felt rather guilty, but then he went on,

"We have no wish for anyone except your father to know where we are going or when we leave. I will call on His Majesty at six o'clock the day after tomorrow. Then on the next morning at daybreak before anyone else in the Palace has risen, we will slip away."

Attila drew in her breath.

"That is such a splendid idea, Father! And you will arrange for the horses?"

"Lamos will do that and if you tell me which horse you wish to ride, he will arrange it."

Attila thought for a moment.

"I think I would prefer Samson to any other horse I am riding at the moment. He is very strong and also very obedient."

"Then Lamos will see to it."

Attila knew that Lamos was a servant who had been with Father Jozsef for many years and he was particularly good with horses.

When Father Jozsef did not need him he helped in the Royal stables.

He was a strong man and if there was any trouble on their journey, he would deal with robbers or anyone else who might try to detain them.

*

When she returned to the Palace she was feeling a great deal happier.

She had been shocked and upset by what her father had told her about his illness, but now she felt certain that if they could reach the Shrine of St. Janos, he would be cured.

She realised the doctors who attended to him would be sceptical of such an idea, but where Father Jozsef and the Saint were concerned miracles *did* happen.

That was just what she expected.

When she walked into luncheon she was not alone with her stepmother.

There was the normal collection of two Ladies-in-Waiting and two Equerries as well as one Member of the Cabinet who had been visiting her father.

As he was good-looking the Queen flirted with the Member of the Cabinet throughout the meal thus making it impossible for anyone else to talk to him.

As the luncheon finished he felt he had neglected Attila.

"I am afraid, Your Royal Highness," he said, "may be finding things a little dull here at the moment. I have not heard of anyone throwing a ball or any other kind of party as it happens."

"I am quite happy without them," replied Attila.

"At the same time it is something I must remedy," the Queen chipped in, "and I think when Prince Otto visits us next week we should have a grand dinner party and a dance afterwards."

The Member of the Cabinet raised his eyebrows.

"Prince Otto of Dedregen. Is he coming here?"

"He has more or less invited himself," the Queen answered, "and of course we cannot possibly refuse him. Personally I find him a charming young man."

The Member of the Cabinet was about to protest that he was anything but charming and then he realised that Attila was beside him.

He obviously thought it would be wrong to mention the scandals surrounding Prince Otto in her presence and Attila was well aware that he had hesitated over what he was about to say.

And then he had bitten back the words.

She thought of saying that she had heard all about the Prince's escapades and therefore she had no wish to meet him, but she thought that as she was going away it would be foolish to cause trouble.

When the Prince did arrive, her stepmother would undoubtedly attempt to make his visit a great success, but fortunately by that time she would be far away on the road to St. Janos!

As they left the dining room table, her stepmother asked,

"What are you doing now, Attila?"

"I am going up to see Papa and if he is asleep, I will not wake him."

She walked away in a hurry as Queen Margit could not think of any reason to prevent her from going to her father.

Attila knew she was afraid that she told the King things about Prince Otto he did not know and if he found out the truth there was every likelihood he would insist on the visit being cancelled.

'My stepmother is so determined to be rid of me,' Attila ruminated as she climbed up the stairs.

Once again she was praying very fervently that her father could be saved and that Father Jozsef and she would be able to prove the doctors wrong.

That would be nothing new as all Valdina's doctors were old-fashioned and very out-of-date where medicine was concerned, although they did their best, but Attila had often thought that far too many people died unnecessarily.

Her mother had constantly believed in the country recipes that had been handed down for generations.

In the past when someone was ill, the White Witch, who existed in most villages, made them a potion from the herbs which grew in the woods and many could be found in the Palace Herb Garden.

They were all simple remedies, but Attila had been given them ever since she was a baby and she had therefore avoided being prescribed for by a doctor.

"If we use the bounty that is given to us by nature or rather by God," her mother had said, "they are far more likely to be effective than anything ever invented by man."

Attila believed this implicitly and she thought now there was every chance that the doctors would be wrong in their diagnosis of her father's condition.

Yet if she said so no one would take any notice of her, least of all her stepmother.

'I am sure if Mama was alive today he would not have become ill,' she thought. 'And as he has never been really happy with his new wife, perhaps that is one of the reasons why he is so ill now.'

It was, however, something she could not say to her father.

She went into his room and found him awake and he seemed delighted to see her.

"Come and talk to me, my dearest," he said. "I am bored with my own company."

"You know that I always love to be with you, Papa. Shall we talk or would you like to play a game of chess?"

"I would like to talk about you," the King said.

"That will bore me. Let us leave things as they are at the moment and let us reminisce about Mama."

The King smiled and she continued,

"Do you remember how happy we were when you taught me to swim in the river? And Mama used to cook a picnic, so we could all be together without a bodyguard or anyone interfering."

The King sighed.

"The sun always seemed to shine and your mother and I were so happy."

"So was I," added Attila.

"I want you to be happy now, my dearest."

"I do think, Papa, that you should pray and believe that you will get well."

"The doctors all say there is nothing they can do for me."

"Do you really think Mama would have listened to them or believed anything they said?"

There was silence for a moment and then the King said,

"No, your mother would have made me a strong concoction of herbs and I would doubtless have been well again in a few days."

"I think that is just what she wants you to be now," Attila told him very softly.

Her father looked at her quizzically.

"Why do you say that?"

"I went to visit Father Jozsef this very morning and I prayed in his little Chapel. I was quite certain, Papa, that Mama was there telling me you had to believe you were going to get well."

She saw her father was listening to her.

"Mama often said the secret of being healed was to believe you would be."

"I can remember her saying that," agreed the King.

"She always said it and I am sure she was right."

"What you are telling me," the King added slowly, "is that I am not to accept what the doctors have said, but believe I shall recover."

"If you believe and that is what Mama would want you to do, I am quite certain you will be well again soon."

She pressed her hand over his.

"You are wanted, wanted desperately by everyone. Do you sincerely believe that I, Stepmama or anyone else could take your place?"

The King drew in his breath.

"It has been worrying me a great deal."

"Do not waste your time and brain worrying, just believe you are going to recover and of course I know, almost as if I can hear her telling you, that is what Mama is praying you will do."

There was silence and Attila knew her father was

thinking of her mother and how much he had loved her.

After what seemed a long time, the King said,

"I will do what you tell me to do, because I know it is what your mother would have wanted. But I have been thinking that if I die, I would be with her and that to me would be Heaven."

"I do not think Mama is far away from any of us, Papa. Equally she would not want you to shirk your duty. As I have always said – Valdina needs you desperately."

"You are quite right, my dearest, and I do admit to being rather feeble in accepting the verdict of those doctors without really querying it."

"They just make it safe for themselves. If you die they will say they predicted it and if you recover they will say it is their brilliance that saved you."

The King laughed as she wanted him to do.

"You are quite right, my dear, that is exactly what they are thinking and I never thought much of them as men let alone as physicians."

"Then forget them and promise me, Papa, that you will say to yourself over and over again, 'I am going to be well, I am going to be well!'"

"Now you are bullying me," he protested. "At the same time because I love you, I will do what you tell me."

Because she knew he would not break his promise, Attila then turned the conversation to other subjects.

They talked of the races they were going to have. One was to be in boats on the river, another would be over the mountains.

In the past the King had always taken part in these races and he had inevitably been the winner.

Attila told him that some people in the country had been training racehorses and intended to challenge him.

This was true to some extent, but she exaggerated it to raise her father's interest as he would have to decide which horses he would enter for the race which was over five miles.

At the end of the race the winner would receive a very handsome trophy.

"I think tomorrow, if you feel strong enough, which I am sure you will be," suggested Attila, "you might order the horses paraded in the garden so that you can see them from the window. There is one special horse I particularly want you to notice."

She went on to describe the horses which had only been brought into the stable since her father's illness.

She knew when she had finished that he was just as interested as he always had been in good horse flesh.

The King would definitely make an effort to sit at the window tomorrow to see his horses and when she left her father he was not as limp as he usually was.

He had talked animatedly to her of the races which had taken place in previous years.

There was a particular one which he and her mother had arranged when Attila was fifteen, when she had raced against children of her own age.

"I cannot think why we ever gave it up," the King muttered.

Attila knew a great many things had been given up or neglected after her mother died, but she thought it would be a mistake to say so.

Instead she urged,

"Hurry up and get well, dear Papa, I have so many new ideas which only you can put into operation. But I am not going to tell you about them now."

"I want to hear them all and if they are for the good

of our people, I must try and find someone interested who will arrange what you want."

"The only one who could arrange anything I want, is you, Papa. You know what old fuddy-duddies they are in Parliament and most of the courtiers say they do not like change."

The King laughed.

"I can hear them saying it!"

"Mama always said that you had the most brilliant ideas and by sheer force of will you made them a success."

"Did she really say that?"

"She told me many times and you know as well as I do, Papa, that if they can put their feet up and grumble 'what was good enough for my grandfather is good enough for me,' that is the attitude of most of them in this Palace."

The King laughed again.

"I can see I shall have to wake them all up, Attila!"

"Of course you must, Papa and the sooner the better or else we shall have moss growing all over the Palace and on the heads of most of the people in it!"

The King kept on laughing.

Just as Attila was going to say more her stepmother came into the room.

"You are not to tire your father, Attila," she began in a scolding tone.

"She is not tiring me," protested the King. "In fact I am feeling better."

There was just a moment's pause before the Queen gushed,

"That is marvellous! But of course you must not do too much. Now lie still and rest. I am sure it is time for you to take your medicine."

The King looked at his daughter and Attila shook her head.

The Queen had walked to a table at the side of the room and poured into a small medicine glass some rather dark concoction the doctor had prepared for him.

She took it to the bedside and handed it to the King.

"Now drink this," she ordered, "and you know we must do exactly as the doctors have told you."

"Oh, look, Stepmama!" exclaimed Attila, "there is that beautiful bird you admired yesterday at the fountain."

Queen Margit turned towards the window.

"Where?" she asked as she reached it.

"It is looking even prettier than when you first saw it," added Attila.

As she spoke she quickly took away the medicine glass the King was holding in his hand.

She emptied it quickly into a vase of flowers on the table next to his bed.

"I cannot see the bird," the Queen grumbled as she turned from the window and walked back to the bed.

The King was holding the empty medicine glass in his hand and she took it from him saying,

"Now you will feel better and don't forget you have to take another glassful before you go to sleep."

The King's eyes were twinkling as he glanced at his daughter.

"I will not forget," he promised.

Attila kissed him saying she would come back and say goodnight to him later.

Then she went to her bedroom and began to decide which clothes she would take with her on her pilgrimage with Father Jozsef.

She knew it would be a mistake to take any of the dresses she wore every day, which were all attractive as her father gave her a large dress allowance and most of them came from the best dressmakers in the City.

They used materials which had been woven in other parts of Europe and sometimes the gowns had particularly lovely embroidery imported from the East.

'As a pilgrim I must look poor,' Attila decided.

There did not seem to be anything at all suitable in her wardrobe and then she suddenly remembered that in the attics there was a vast collection of clothes left by every generation.

They had been kept just in case they came in useful and her mother had often laughed and said that one day they would be able to open a fashion museum.

She obtained the key from the housekeeper and said firmly she did not need her to accompany her as she was only looking for a small item she felt might be stored there.

The attics, which fortunately were dry, were packed with different clothes.

In one room there was the uniform and riding boots worn by her grandfather as well as his evening clothes and even those he wore at his Coronation.

One complete attic was given over to the previous Kings, but there were many more rooms for everything that had been left behind by the Queens.

Their wedding dresses and all the many gowns they wore at Court and in mourning were hanging up neatly.

Attila passed from room to room seeing nothing but heavy embroidery, ermine and furs. There were trains she was sure required at least three stalwart pages to carry.

Finally she stopped at one dingy small room where things were different.

It took Attila a little time to remember that one of her great-aunts who never married became very religious as she grew older.

She recalled being told how Great-Aunt Louisa had visited Churches and Shrines all over Europe.

Attila looked around carefully to find that her aunt had worn a number of garments which she considered to be correct for a pilgrim.

In fact, some of her clothes were very like those of a nun, except that they were actually made of much more expensive materials.

Strangely enough they were rather becoming when Attila tried them on.

What she did admire was a cape her great-aunt had clearly covered herself with when she was travelling and attached to it was a little hood which she could pull down over her face.

She picked up two capes besides a number of plain dresses with long sleeves and by the time she had finished looking round, she had a nice pile of clothes to take down to her bedroom.

Then she remembered that if she did so, her lady's maid would surely wonder why she required them, so she took another look round the attics and found just what she expected.

There were big stacks of old trunks, cases and even some bags.

She managed to squeeze everything she had chosen into a bag and a case and carried them downstairs without asking the help of any of the pages.

She put them in the bedroom next to her own which was not in use as she felt no one would notice them there.

When she finally returned to her own room it was time for her to have her bath before dinner.

*

Later that night she went to say goodnight to her father.

When she entered the room, the blinds were drawn and there was still a lighted candle by his bedside.

"I thought you would come to see me, my dearest," he said when Attila appeared. "I want you to throw away these sleeping draughts the doctors always give me. I am certain after what you said it makes me feel drowsy in the morning."

Attila picked up the glass and taking it to the open window, she emptied it into the garden.

"You know that Mama always said if you could not sleep, you should take a little honey."

"I had forgotten her excellent advice and when the doctors insisted their medicine was good for me, I believed them."

"I am certain their sleeping draughts make you feel muzzy, as you have just said, and they are also very bad for your brain, Papa."

"You are quite right, my dearest, and I will not take one again. In fact after our talk this afternoon I feel better already."

Attila hugged him.

"You are so sensible and intelligent, Papa. How could you possibly think those stupid men could ever know better than Mama?"

"I am going to get well, *I am going to get well*," the King recited.

Attila hugged him again.

"That is so right, Papa, you have always got what you wanted even if you have had to fight for it. So you *will* win this battle."

"I am certainly going to try and that, incidentally, is something I had not thought of before."

"You *will* win," Attila prophesised and kissed him again.

CHAPTER THREE

The butler knocked on the King's bedroom door.

"Come in," he called.

"Father Jozsef, Your Majesty."

The King pushed himself a little higher up in bed.

"I was much looking forward to seeing you, Father Jozsef," he greeted him.

They shook hands and Father Jozsef sat down on a chair beside the bed.

"How is Your Majesty?"

"Feeling better because I am delighted to see you. My daughter is telling me that your garden is even better this year and that is saying a great deal!"

Father Jozsef laughed.

"Her Royal Highness is right. I work very hard on it and I know if you come to see it, Your Majesty will be impressed."

"That is something I intend to do as soon as I can."

There was a short silence then Father Jozsef said,

"I have something to tell Your Majesty."

The King looked rather apprehensive.

"I am taking Her Royal Highness away tomorrow morning, as she desires to make a pilgrimage to St. Janos on Your Majesty's behalf."

The King looked at Father Jozsef in astonishment.

"A pilgrimage," he exclaimed.

"Princess Attila believes in prayer as I do and we both pray for a miracle where Your Majesty is concerned."

"As it so happens I am feeling a little better because Attila has told me I was making a huge mistake in taking the medicine and sleeping draughts the doctors have given me."

"I am sure the Princess is quite right."

"I was very foolish, Father, in not consulting you. I am sure you have cured more people in your time than any of these doctors who give themselves such airs."

"That is a subject I would wish to talk to you about, Your Majesty, as well as the pilgrimage Princess Attila and I are undertaking."

"Are you sure it will not be too much for you?"

"I am convinced that nothing is more important to Valdina than that Your Majesty should be on the throne."

The King was well aware by the way Father Jozsef spoke that he knew the Queen desired the throne if he died.

It was a matter, however, that he felt he should not discuss with the Father, so he merely said,

"If you really believe, Father, that a pilgrimage to St. Janos will give me back my health, then I am prepared to leave my daughter in your charge."

"I will take the greatest care of her, Your Majesty, and I think that you are aware that she has another reason for leaving the Palace at this time."

The King gave the Father a sharp glance.

"Are you referring to the visit of Prince Otto?"

He knew as he spoke it was somewhat indiscreet to discuss a Royal guest, but Father Jozsef had always been a privileged person.

As the King realised there were few secrets which were not known to him.

"Since Your Majesty has mentioned him, I can only say that if our beloved Queen Anna was still alive, Prince Otto would never be allowed to cross the threshold of the Palace."

The King raised his eyebrows.

"Is he as bad as that?" he enquired. "I really know very little about him."

"He is someone, Your Majesty, who should never come into contact with any decent woman and certainly not a young girl who knows very little of the world."

The King drew in his breath.

He recognised that it was really impossible to query anything that Father Jozsef said, but he had no wish at this moment to be involved in a long argument with the Queen.

After all she invited Prince Otto and she must have had some idea what his reputation was like.

"If what you have just said is the truth, as of course it is, Father, then I am most grateful to you for taking Attila away."

"Because the Princess has no wish to upset anyone, we have agreed between us that the only person who shall know where we have gone and why is Your Majesty.

"We are in fact leaving at dawn tomorrow morning and we would be grateful if no one was informed that we are missing until we are some way away from the Palace."

The King smiled.

"I can see you have thought it all out very carefully and of course you are right. It is always wise to go quickly and avoid explanations."

"That is just what Princess Attila felt and therefore no one will have the slightest idea of what has happened to her except Your Majesty."

"I am so glad I have been let into your secret, but I cannot believe you are making your pilgrimage on foot."

"That is correct," replied Father Jozsef, "because as Your Majesty well knows I am not as young as I was."

His eyes were twinkling as he added,

"My carriage where the Princess will sleep is drawn by two excellent stallions from the Royal stables. We are also taking a mount for me and Samson, which I gather is Her Royal Highness's favourite mount."

The King threw back his head and laughed.

"I might well have guessed, Father, that you would choose the best and you are right to do so. I understand from what you have just told me you have no wish to take a Royal Guard with you."

"Certainly not, Your Majesty. We are just two very unimportant people to whom no one will give a second glance going on a pilgrimage to the Shrine of St. Janos."

"I can see how well you two have thought it all out, Father. You have my full approval and I promise you no one will guess where you and Attila are, but I shall be quite content because she is in your hands."

"There is something else I would now wish to say to Your Majesty about yourself."

"I am listening, Father."

"I expect Your Majesty will have heard of Salem, the village which is about ten miles from here?"

"Yes, it is a small village with a large lake."

"That is right, but I do not know if Your Majesty is aware that the people of Salem are the healthiest people in the whole country!"

"If I was told it, I cannot remember it."

"Well, they are, and what is so strange is that there has never been any illness to any of the people of Salem. When their ages were last counted there were three men of over a hundred years of age and a large number of men and women nearing ninety."

The King stared at him.

"Is there any reason for it?"

"The reason I believe comes from the water in the lake and the land where the locals grow their food."

"Surely that is nothing unusual?" asked the King.

"I know of no other place where the people are so healthy and where those who join them are cured of many different diseases."

The King now realised that this information was of interest to himself.

He was listening intently as Father Jozsef went on,

"Two years ago I sent two young chimney sweeps to Salem, suffering from a strange growth on their skin due to their being continually in contact with soot."

"And they were cured?"

"Completely and the same applied to the workers in a tar factory who spent several weeks there bathing in the lake and drinking the water. The growths on their skin had vanished completely before they left."

"I do know why you are telling me this, Father, but apparently the growths which the doctors think are fatal are somewhere, I gather, near my heart."

"I sent a woman to Salem six months ago, who had unceasing pain in one of her breasts. The doctors told her it was a growth of some sort, but they had no idea how to cure it and she left them with no hope."

"And what happened to her?"

"She returned after only three weeks to her family, saying that the pain had left her. She was quite convinced that she was completely cured of whatever was hurting her and making her so miserable."

There was silence before the King asked,

"Are you seriously suggesting that I go to Salem?"

"I think it would be very difficult for Your Majesty, but as I am convinced it is the water of Salem which works these miracles, I see no reason why the waters cannot be brought to the Palace in bottles, so that you drink it and in large containers so that you can bathe in it."

"Father, you are a magician! And of course I will do as you suggest."

"I also believe that the vegetables grown in Salem and the animals which come to the lake must be influenced by what they eat and drink, so Your Majesty should now purchase your meals for the next month or so from Salem."

The King realised there was no real difficulty about the Father's suggestion. He only had to give the order to his chefs.

"I must thank you very humbly, Father, for giving me hope when I thought the only thing left for me was to say my prayers and die."

"I hope Your Majesty will still say your prayers and of course Princess Attila and I will be praying for you at St. Janos's Shrine. I am absolutely convinced in my mind that all our prayers will be answered, but they will certainly be helped by everything Your Majesty obtains from Salem."

"I thank you more than I can put into words," said the King, "you have given me hope and that at times is something very hard to come by."

"I think what is more important that anything else, if I may say so, Your Majesty, is that you should be back ruling your people and leading them into the prosperity this country so richly deserves."

Father Jozsef rose to his feet.

"Before you leave, I would ask for your blessing,

Father. It is something you have given me ever since I was young and I have never failed to be grateful for it."

Father Jozsef smiled and putting his hands together he said a prayer and blessed the King.

Only as he reached the door did he turn back to say,

"Your Majesty will not forget, please, that no one is to know about Princess Attila's and my secret."

"Cross my very heart, I will keep it absolutely and completely to myself," the King promised.

He was certain when the Father had left that he had given him hope just as Attila had done.

In addition he had most skilfully, without upsetting anyone but the Queen, arranged to spirit Attila away before Prince Otto arrived.

Now he thought about Otto the King found it hard to understand.

How could the Queen even contemplate marrying his precious daughter to a man for whom apparently no one had a good word?

He decided, however, he would not make any fuss about it as Attila would have already disappeared.

Therefore whatever festivities were arranged for the visit of Prince Otto, she would not be around to participate in them.

When Attila came to kiss him goodnight he said in a low voice,

"I think really, my dearest, you are saying goodbye to me for quite some time."

"Father Jozsef and I are going to pray for you and I know, Papa, that you will get well."

The King had already given his orders to bring food and water from Salem as Father Jozsef had suggested.

He did not discuss it with Attila merely saying,

"I am so very grateful to you for undertaking this pilgrimage on my behalf and I just cannot believe that your prayers and those of Father Jozsef will not be answered."

"I expect as soon as I return I shall be able to ride with you again, Papa, and there is a new horse which I am sure you will find irresistible."

"I shall be looking forward to it and do take care of yourself, my precious daughter."

"Father Jozsef will be doing it for me and I expect because I am travelling with him that there will be a dozen invisible angels hovering over us."

The King laughed.

"I am certain you are right and because it is such an important pilgrimage, I am only surprised that you are not flying to the Shrine on angels' wings!"

Attila laughed and hugged him.

"I knew you would understand, Papa, and not make a fuss because I am going alone with Father Jozsef. If we had other people with us, it would spoil the pilgrimage and make it difficult for us to concentrate on you."

"I shall be thinking about you all the time you are away, my dearest Attila, and carrying out yours and Father Jozsef's instructions to the letter."

Attila kissed him affectionately before going to her own bedroom.

She knew that the King was better already because he was not taking the doctors' medicine and because Father Jozsef would have blessed him.

'I cannot think why we waited so long and listened to what those stupid doctors had to say,' she said to herself. 'It is all my fault, I should have remembered Mama's herbs earlier and not been frightened by the doctors.'

It took her some time to go to sleep.

*

As she had not drawn back her bedroom curtains, the first gleam of light in the sky woke her.

It was dawn and Father Jozsef would be waiting for her.

After her lady's maid had left her last night, Attila had put out the clothes she was going to wear to travel in.

She had carried in her large bag and case from the bedroom next door and dressed herself in the clothes she had found in the attic.

Then holding on to her luggage she crept out of her bedroom and down the stairs. There was no one about and she unbolted one of the doors into the garden.

It was not difficult to find her way across the lawn and under the trees.

She was, however, glad when she reached the little valley where Father Jozsef's Chapel was situated.

Attila had only taken a few steps when Kilkos, the young man who was travelling with them, came running up to her and took the case and bag from Attila.

Then they hurried along the twisting path which led towards the Chapel.

There was no time for her to go into the Chapel this morning and beyond Father Jozsef's garden she could see that there was a carriage drawn by two horses with Lamos already holding the reins.

Father Jozsef was standing beside the two horses he and Attila were to ride and before she reached him, Kilkos had already put their luggage into the back of the carriage.

Attila greeted Father Jozsef and then Kilkos helped her on to the saddle of Samson.

She bent forward to give the stallion she loved an affectionate pat and she thought that he was as excited as she was about the unexpected adventure.

Father Jozsef mounted the other horse which was almost as handsome as Samson and Kilkos sprang up onto the box of the carriage and they were off.

Father Jozsef led the way followed by Attila and as it was so early there was no one to see them riding through the quiet streets near the Palace.

Very shortly they were out into wide country where there were no people and no horses. There was only wild grassland which slipped away into an indefinite horizon.

They were riding in an area Attila knew resembled the Steppes of Hungary.

The horses needed no encouragement to gallop and as Attila rode every day, she found no difficulty in riding in a plain long garment rather than her riding habit.

She forgot about herself as they galloped over the high grass filled with many teeming wild flowers on which the butterflies were beginning to flutter.

As the sun came up, its rays touched the tops of the mountain on one side of them and shimmered on the river which ran for many miles through the grassland ahead.

It was only when they galloped for what seemed to Attila a long time that she spoke to Father Jozsef.

"We have got away, Father," she said with a note of triumph in her voice.

Father Jozsef smiled at her.

"As you have said," he replied, "we have got away. By the time they want to send a search party for us we will be in a different world where no one will find us."

"I am sure Papa will tell them I am quite safe and with friends, which is, of course, true."

Father Jozsef looked around him.

"I had almost forgotten how very beautiful this part of the country is and our carriage is not far behind us."

The carriage was moving along a rough track at the side of the river as they rode on.

As the sun rose everything around them seemed to be shining and turned to gold.

Everywhere Attila looked there was a profusion of even more butterflies, which rose in front of the horses like an elusive cloud.

The birds they disturbed soared up into the sky and she felt that each one carried a special prayer for her father.

They stopped at noon for luncheon and by that time Attila who had eaten no breakfast was feeling hungry.

The horses were watered and Lamos brought two picnic baskets out from the back of the carriage.

The food was simple, but because she was hungry Attila found it delicious.

She enjoyed talking to Father Jozsef while they ate and drank.

To her considerable surprise he had brought a light wine with him and the men had cooled it in the river.

"I never believed you would drink wine, Father!" exclaimed Attila.

"I very seldom do, but as I thought I might need something to sustain me on a long journey, I considered it a wise precaution against you having to ride alone!"

Attila gave a little cry.

"You must not overtire yourself, Father. You can quite easily drive in the carriage and I can ride beside you."

"I am happy as things are at the moment, my child, but if I feel it is too much for me I shall be sensible enough to say so. As you will know I have promised your father to protect you and that means I cannot leave you alone."

"No, of course not," agreed Attila, "and it is very wonderful of you to come with me."

"You would certainly not be allowed to go alone," commented Father Jozsef sternly.

Attila knew this was very true and what was more if her stepmother had known what was about to happen she would have prevented her from leaving the Palace.

'I have just escaped,' she mused gleefully. 'I have escaped not only to save my Papa, but to save myself from Prince Otto.'

Even to think about him made her shudder so she changed the subject and talked to Father Jozsef about the countryside.

*

That evening they took their second meal of the day in a far more secluded place.

They stopped by a large wood and for the first time Attila looked inside their carriage. It was wide and well padded, but what Attila had not expected was that Father Jozsef had divided it very skilfully down the middle.

There was enough room for two people to sleep on the floor at the same time. The seats had been taken out and the floor was covered with two thick and comfortable mattresses.

There was one on each side of a long wooden board which divided the carriage completely into two tiny rooms.

Attila looked at the side where she was to sleep and she was touched to find a small mirror fixed to the wall as well as a little shelf for her brushes.

"How clever of you!" she cried to Father Jozsef.

He proudly showed her his side, which was almost the same as hers.

There was a place for his razor and toothbrush in front of the mirror and hooks for their clothes.

Attila thought it was the cleverest transformation of a driving carriage she could ever have imagined.

"Where will the two men sleep?" she asked.

"They will sleep underneath the carriage and they have brought sleeping bags with them."

Father Jozsef sighed before he added,

"It is something I would have done myself if I was young, but I thought it wiser to be beside you. Also at my age I am rather bad at crawling under anything!"

Attila laughed.

"Of course you must not and I do think our moving Palace is delightful."

They rode until the sun was beginning to slip down the sky and then it was time for their supper.

This time Lamos insisted on building a fire.

They had hot soup to start with which Attila found delicious.

She and Father Jozsef were seated at some distance from the fire and the men who waited on them and when they had finished the wine which Father Jozsef had insisted she drank, Attila commented,

"I have been thinking, Father, how lucky I am that you have taken me away from the Palace so that I will not have to meet Prince Otto."

"I hope you never meet him, my child."

"That is what I hope too, but I am sure Stepmama will find another suitor she will force me to marry simply because she wants to be rid of me."

"You have not forgotten that one of our reasons for going to the Shrine at St. Janos is to pray that you will find love."

"I have *not* forgotten, Father."

There was a short silence and then she enquired,

"Have you ever been in love, Father?"

He looked at her quizzically and Attila thought he was debating whether he would tell her the truth.

He might make an excuse to talk about something else, but he answered her,

"The reason I entered the Church and became as I am today was because I loved someone with all my heart, but I lost her."

"How did that happen? Surely she did not have to marry someone else."

Father Jozsef shook his head.

"No, no. I loved her and she loved me, but we were both very young. I had no money and there was no chance of us marrying until I could provide her a proper home."

"Your father was not well-off?"

"He had a little money and later made a great deal more, but I was just one of a family of six. Actually as my brothers were older, my father had enabled them to acquire homes which cost him a considerable amount of money."

"So you were going to marry the girl you loved so much when you could afford it, Father."

"That was more or less the situation except that her father wanted her to marry someone much more important and certainly richer than I was."

"But she loved you," questioned Attila.

"She loved me," Father Jozsef repeated, "and our love was the real love, which you, my dear Princess, are seeking."

"Then what happened?"

There was silence as if the Father could not bear to speak about it. Eventually he replied,

"She contracted a fever for which there was no cure in those days."

"Are you saying," she whispered, "that she died?"

"She died in my arms, telling me with her very last breath that she loved me."

The way he spoke made tears come to Attila's eyes.

"I am sorry, so very sorry, Father."

"Now you understand," he continued with a tremor in his voice, "why I then entered the Church and dedicated my life to helping others not only spiritually, but, when I was able, physically."

"I wondered why you knew so much about illness. So many, many people must be grateful to you."

"Every time I heal someone, I think it could have happened to the one I loved so much. If only I had known not only about medicine, but the power of prayer."

"You have done so much good for the world, but it is very, very sad that you lost the girl you loved. What was her name?"

"She had the same name as the beloved Mother of Christ, but I called her – Marie."

"Wherever Marie is now, she must be very proud of how saintly you are and the many people you have healed."

Father Jozsef rose to his feet and walked away.

Attila knew he wanted to be alone, as he wished to think of Marie who he had loved.

There could never be another woman in his life.

He was a Priest and entirely on his own and there was no one to share his work or his thoughts with him.

'It is very, very sad,' thought Attila. 'But if it had not happened many others would have suffered. Without Father Jozsef to heal them they would have died or perhaps never known love.'

At the same time her heart bled for Father Jozsef.

She wanted desperately for him to be happy.

When she went to bed he still had not returned from his walk and Attila worried in case he was doing too much.

When she heard him return and enter the carriage, she was relieved.

She was tired and fell asleep immediately.

*

She only awakened when she heard Father Jozsef moving about and the horses being put between the shafts.

When they set off again it was another lovely day.

Now Attila felt more relaxed.

Yesterday, although she told herself it was totally unnecessary, she kept glancing over her shoulder just in case there were soldiers following them.

She tried not to think that her stepmother would be so very angry when she found she had disappeared and she was quite capable, without discussing it with her father, of sending the Palace guards in search of her.

They were now leaving the grassland behind them, but the air was still filled with birds and butterflies.

At noon on the third day of their journey Attila saw a tall mountain ahead, where the Shrine of St. Janos was situated.

As they drew nearer there were one or two pilgrims just like themselves. They were either walking slowly as if they had travelled from a long distance or riding a horse or donkey.

Most of the pilgrims seemed to be young and she thought that perhaps like herself they were going to the Shrine to ask for love.

They reached the mountain and they could only go

a little way up on horseback and then the rough track came to an end.

There was a place at the side of the mountain where the carriage and horses could stand.

It was then, looking at the steep path ahead of them, that Attila approached Father Jozsef,

"You are really certain, Father, that it will not be too much for you?"

He smiled at her.

"I will be alright if I take it slowly, my child. After all we have come a long way to pray at the Shrine and I do not want my prayers to be in vain."

Attila shook her head.

"I am certain they never can be, Father, wherever you make them."

"That is true, but I am anxious for you to see the Shrine which I think is very beautiful. You will find it has a wonderful feeling all of its own which there is no need for me to describe to you."

Attila was becoming very excited now that they had reached their journey's end.

She tidied herself in the mirror in the carriage and put on a fresh gown.

It was very different to the smart attractive dresses she wore at home, but she felt it was appropriate

She was only a humble pilgrim at the feet of a Saint who had proved himself a thousand times.

She insisted on Father Jozsef having a glass of his wine before they began to climb the steep path ahead.

When she had drunk it for the second time last night she suspected it was not an ordinary wine like those which were served at her father's table.

"What have you added to it, Father?" she asked.

"That is clever of you, my child," he answered her. "How do you know I have added anything?"

"I can taste it and I can feel that it has an uplifting feeling when I drink it which sweeps away tiredness."

"That is just what you are meant to feel. Actually it contains many herbs that are stimulating when added to the grapes when it is brewed."

"So you have it specially made for you, Father?"

"I have given my recipe to a friend who I believe has made a fortune from it, but I drink very little myself, although he sends me a case every time I require one."

"Then I am so delighted we have tasted it on this journey and if you feel stimulated by it, Father, so do I. To tell you the truth I was feeling very tired last night."

"I thought you were and that is why I insisted on you having a glass at supper time."

Attila reached out to touch his hand.

"You are so kind to me, Father, and I am sure Papa is envying me coming here with you and perhaps when he is better he will want to go on a pilgrimage himself."

They put down their glasses and leaving the horses and the carriage in the charge of the two men, they started to walk very slowly up the path.

They could not see very much before they reached the top and when they did so Attila thought it was certainly worth the effort.

The Shrine had been altered several times over the years to make it more and more impressive.

It was in a small clearing standing on the stones of the mountain and been built very much higher than it had been originally.

Now it was covered with a roof of gold and silver

and there were candles made of gold and inset with jewels burning on each side.

These had been a present from an Indian Maharajah who had claimed that the Saint had given him five million blessings, and he had received an answer to his prayers that no temple in his own country had been able to do.

On the other side of the Shrine and below it there was another building where the guards slept.

Father Jozsef had told Attila that there were quite a number of Priests and students always in attendance.

There were many offerings surrounding the Shrine that had been brought by pilgrims from all over the world and some were very valuable.

It was, however, completely impossible to think of ordinary problems when one came near to the Shrine.

Attila was instinctively aware of the extraordinary and unusual atmosphere around it.

When she knelt down beside Father Jozsef she felt as if the Shrine itself was reaching out to her and calling her to give her very heart and soul in her prayers.

The Shrine also assured her that her prayers would be answered.

She could not explain this even to herself and yet the feeling was strong and overwhelming.

She felt as if she had stepped into Heaven and was no longer on earth.

Attila closed her eyes and started to pray.

She prayed for her father not only for his health but for his happiness.

Then without even thinking of what she was doing she found herself praying that he would be saved from her stepmother and that she would not be able to harm him or make him unhappy.

She could not quite understand why these thoughts were so prevalent with her at his moment and yet she was so sure they were a vital part of her prayers.

She could not ignore them and it was almost, she thought, as if someone was telling her that her father was in danger.

Not from his health but from his wife.

Attila must have prayed for quite a long time.

Then, as she thought she would rise, she turned first to look at Father Jozsef.

He was beside her and she wondered if his prayers too were finished and he was ready to leave.

He was kneeling with his back very straight and his head high.

At first glance she could see that his eyes were not closed.

He was looking at the Shrine and the Cross which stood on top of it.

She bent towards him to ask in a whisper if he was ready to rise.

Suddenly he threw out his arms and in a voice that vibrated with a wild excitement, he exclaimed,

"Marie! Marie! Marie!"

He called out her name three times.

Then he fell forward.

As he did so and just before he touched the ground, Attila knew that he had joined Marie who he had loved all through the years.

As three guards hurried forward, she knew in her heart that he was dead.

CHAPTER FOUR

The guards carried Father Jozsef's body out of the Shrine and took it down to the Monastery where they lived.

Following them Attila was not surprised that there was a small Chapel attached to the Monastery and Father Jozsef was taken inside and laid down in front of the altar.

Then one of the guards asked her who he was.

"He is Father Jozsef from Valdina."

The guards looked at her in some surprise and she realised that they had heard of the Father, but they had not expected him to come to the Shrine as a pilgrim.

They took Attila into another room and asked her to wait while they went to fetch the Father Superior.

He was a distinguished looking elderly man and the guards bowed him into the room where Attila was waiting.

"I hear," he now began, "that Father Jozsef, whom we have all loved and admired, has passed on to God."

"I think," said Attila quietly with tears in her eyes, "it is just what he himself wanted, because as he died he saw the woman he had always loved."

"That is exactly what I have understood from my men and I suppose you are with him as a pupil."

"He brought me on this pilgrimage," Attila replied. "I am most concerned about my father's health and I also have a private wish of my own, which Father Jozsef felt St. Janos would answer for me."

"I am quite sure he was right, my child, but how are you to return to Valdina?"

"There is no trouble about that, because I came here on horseback and Father Jozsef rode too. His two servants brought his carriage for us to sleep in."

"Then that does solve one problem," said the Father Superior with a smile. "Otherwise I would send a guard to accompany you on your return to Valdina."

"That is so kind of you, Father, but it will be quite unnecessary. Lamos has been with Father Jozsef for many years and will, I know, look after me as if he was still with us."

"Which I am sure he will be."

The Father Superior asked Attila to wait while they attended to Father Jozsef and then he asked,

"Do you wish to take Father Jozsef back with you to his own country? Or shall we bury him here?"

Attila looked surprised and he explained,

"Several people have asked if they could be buried close to the Shrine and others, just like Father Jozsef, have succumbed owing to the long journey."

Attila thought for a moment.

"I think that as Father Jozsef had such a respect and devotion to the Shrine, he would rather be buried here than at home."

"Then we shall be very honoured to have him. His healing powers and the help he has given to so many has aroused a great admiration amongst those who worship at the Shrine and we would be happy for his body to remain with us."

"Then I am sure that is what he would want too," added Attila.

The Father Superior left her to give his instructions and Attila sat down to wait for his return.

She had made a significant decision when she was walking behind the guards carrying Father Jozsef.

It would be a grave mistake for her to say who she was as someone in charge would insist on arranging for her to be escorted back to the Palace because she was a Royal.

'I will just return quietly by myself with Lamos and Kilkos,' she decided. 'I want to think and have no wish to take strangers with me or, for that matter, an armed guard.'

When the Father Superior returned, he took her into the little Chapel where Father Jozsef had already been put into a simple coffin.

There were two large candles burning on each side of it and flowers on the floor.

Attila looked at Father Jozsef as she had not been able to do previously and there was a radiance in his face which she had never seen before.

She realised it was because his soul had been united with the woman he had always loved.

She knelt down beside his coffin and prayed that he should bless her as he had done when he was alive.

She begged him to bring her eventually to the same happiness he had found.

The young Priest who was attending on her told her that Father Jozsef's funeral would take place at dawn the next morning.

"We will take it in turns to pray here tonight," he said, "but the Father Superior thought you would wish to return to those who are with you before darkness sets in."

"That is very gracious of His Reverence and I hope he will permit me to bring Father Jozsef's two servants, not only to the Chapel to see him, but to attend the funeral."

"The Father Superior has thought of that and two of our men will care for your horses while they are away."

Attila thought that no one could be kinder or more considerate.

She spent a long time praying beside Father Jozsef in the Chapel.

Then, as Lamos and Kilkos would not have heard what had occurred, she went back to the carriage and told them that Father Jozsef had left them.

There were tears in both their eyes and Lamos said,

"It was the way Father Jozsef would have liked to have gone. He was afraid of being decrepit like some of the people he treated. Several times he said to me 'I want to die while I am still active and my brain functions as it should do'."

"He was granted his wish," added Attila wistfully.

She did not inform them that he had called out for Marie, as she felt that was a very personal matter and they would not have known her in the first place.

She was only glad that Father Jozsef had told her all about Marie.

It merely confirmed what she had always believed that there is no such thing as death and it was a great truth Father Jozsef had told her when she was very small.

If she had needed confirmation nothing could have been more miraculous than the joy in his voice as he died and the radiance on his face.

Now the two lovers, separated from each other for so long, were together again.

'That is the love I want. Please God give it to me,' Attila prayed when she went back to the Chapel.

The Monks had brought in more flowers and there were candles on the altar and round the coffin.

Attila knelt down quietly at the altar as the young men who served at the Shrine were coming in to kneel and say a prayer.

She had a strong feeling each of them went away believing they had been blessed by Father Jozsef.

The sun was sinking lower in the sky.

So she now returned to the place where Lamos and Kilkos were waiting for her.

Attila did not feel like talking, so she ate the dinner which Lamos had prepared for her alone by the fireside.

Then as darkness began to fall she went to bed in the carriage.

It was then, for the first time, that she wept copious tears because she had lost Father Jozsef.

She knew that no one could ever replace him in her life as he was not only her spiritual teacher but her friend.

'There is no one else I can talk to as freely,' she told herself, 'or who would understand what I feel before I can even put it into words.'

Then almost as if someone was providing her with the answer, she knew that when she found love she would no longer be alone.

*

She slept a little and woke when it was daybreak.

The Father Superior had said that the funeral was to take place at eight o'clock before any pilgrims were likely to climb up to the Shrine.

Attila, accompanied by Lamos and Kelkos, climbed up the steep path that had so exhausted Father Jozsef only yesterday and reached the Shrine.

They stopped for a moment to pray and then Attila led them down to the Monastery.

Even as they arrived a procession was coming out of the small Chapel. There were six stalwart young Priests carrying the coffin followed by number of mourners, who were singing and bearing flowers.

Attila walked behind the Father Superior.

They processed for a little way along the side of the mountain until they came to another clearing, which had been made by removing the very stones themselves.

It was a small perfectly kept graveyard with about ten graves each one with a marble cross bearing the name of the occupant.

The grave for Father Jozsef had been prepared and he was lowered gently into it by the six Priests who had carried his coffin.

Then the Father Superior began the Service for the Dead.

His voice was deep and the sincere way he spoke was, Attila thought, very moving.

Holy Water was now sprinkled on the coffin before it was covered and the assembled company sang a psalm.

As they sang two small serving boys wearing lace-edged surplices joined them swinging incense holders in their hands.

As the psalm came to an end, Attila walked forward and placed a bouquet of lilies on top of the coffin.

There were a few more prayers and then the monks covered the coffin with earth and the flowers were placed on top of the grave.

Attila felt he would have been pleased and glad that he lay beneath them and her lilies were at his breast.

Finally everyone knelt down for the Father Superior to bless them.

He said he was certain the blessing he was giving them was coming from Father Jozsef as well. They would never forget him and he would never forget them and his words about Father Jozsef brought tears to Attila's eyes.

The Service ended and for several minutes no one moved.

The Father Superior came to Attila's side and held out his hand helping her to rise.

"You have been very brave, my child, and I know Father Jozsef would be proud of you."

"I am sure he is happy to lie here with you, Father."

He smiled at Attila.

"Now I think you should go home. It is a long way to Valdina and I am quite sure your father will be waiting for you and because of Father Jozsef's prayers and mine he will be in better health than when you left him."

"Thank you, Father, and please go on praying for Papa as it is so very important that he should live and be strong."

"I will not forget him," he assured her.

Attila walked back with Lamos and Kilkos and they stopped for a moment at the Shrine where now there was a crowd of pilgrims.

Then they climbed down to where their horses and the carriage were waiting.

Attila gave the guards who had looked after them a generous gift which they appreciated.

She wondered when she reached home whether she should write a letter to the Father Superior telling him who she was and she was sure that her father would give him a generous donation for the Shrine.

She knew it was only the money collected from the pilgrims and donations from those who could afford it that supported the Monastery.

She mounted Samson and he nuzzled against her in delight.

Lamos drove the carriage and Kilkos rode Father Jozsef's horse and he was tactful and well trained enough to keep a little behind Attila, so she could feel free to enjoy the beauty of the grassland.

They covered a little more mileage than they had on the way out and they only stopped for a very short time for something to eat at midday.

They were now in a part of the country where there were no houses or any sign of human habitation.

It was Lamos who, thinking the horses had gone far enough, found a place for them to rest in a beautiful spot with a thick wood on one side of them.

The grassland with its endless birds and butterflies stretched as far as one could see into a distant horizon and there was a small stream running from the wood which was excellent for the horses.

When Lamos released them from the shafts of the carriage and took off their harness, they rolled happily in the grassland and galloped off to the stream to drink.

Samson joined them and Attila knew that he was so well-trained that he would come back if she called him.

Lamos and Kilkos started to build a fire and Attila appreciated that they would have procured enough fresh food from the Monastery for them not to go hungry.

She sat a little bit way from the fire thinking how beautiful the flames were, rising against the darkness of the trees.

She wished she had someone to talk to.

She had so enjoyed the meals she had shared with Father Jozsef as he always had such interesting things to say to her.

She knew that if she had been with her father there would have been many topics on which they would both have very definite opinions.

Lamos was cooking something in a saucepan over the fire and from the smell Attila guessed her meal would start with a soup with many different ingredients.

Lamos, as it happened, was a very good cook and she noticed that Kilkos had been sent to find mushrooms growing in the moss.

Quite suddenly a man riding very swiftly came out of the wood and headed towards them.

Attila watched him in surprise because he appeared to be in such a hurry.

When he reached her, he pulled in his horse and shouted,

"For God's sake hide me *or I am a dead man.*"

Attila sprang to her feet.

Almost as if she was being guided, she knew what to do.

The young man flung himself off his horse.

Kilkos dropped his mushrooms and ran to Attila as if she had called him.

"Take off his saddle and bridle," she ordered him.

And to the young man standing beside her she said,

"Come with me."

She ran towards the carriage.

As he followed her he was looking apprehensively towards the wood which he had just come from.

"They are right behind me," he muttered, "and they intend to kill me."

Attila did not answer.

She merely opened the door of the carriage on the side where Father Jozsef had slept.

As she expected a cassock was hanging by the bed.

"Put this on quickly," she urged. "Then lie down as if you are asleep and shave away your moustache."

The young man did exactly as he was told.

He put on Father Jozsef's cassock, pulled the hood over his head and climbed into the carriage.

Attila closed the door and walked back to the fire.

She noted that Kilkos had obeyed her instructions and the horse free of its saddle and bridle was trotting away to join the other horses in the stream.

She sat down where she had been sitting earlier.

She thought that this was the most extraordinary experience that had ever happened to her.

Then out of the wood in the same place where the young man had appeared came four men on horseback.

The leader galloped up to her.

As she looked up at him, he called at her sharply in a language she only just understood,

"A man came this way, where is he?"

Attila thought he had an unpleasant face, although he was broad-shouldered and could have been quite good-looking.

But there was something mean about his eyes and she felt instinctively he was not to be trusted.

"There is no man here," she replied firmly.

Then pointing towards the way they had just come, she told him,

"There are a number of pilgrims going to the Shrine of St. Janos."

"I am not interested in pilgrims," he snapped, "only a man on horseback."

As he was speaking two more rough-looking men joined him while the third stayed by the wood.

They were looking to right and left searching for the man Attila had just hidden.

"I was sure he would come through this way," said the leader. "Are those your horses by the stream?"

"Yes, they are ours," responded Attila.

"There are five and only three of you!"

He was looking towards Lamos and Kilkos.

Attila knew the answer.

"Father Jozsef is not well," she said. "He is asleep in the carriage."

He dismounted.

"I want to look at him," he said aggressively.

For a moment Attila felt her heart stop beating and then she replied,

"He is asleep. He has been very ill and the reason we visited the Shrine was to pray for his recovery."

"All the same I wish to take a look at him," the man retorted in a truculent voice.

"Very well then, but as he is asleep you are not to disturb him."

He was already walking towards the carriage and there was nothing Attila could do but go with him.

At the same time she was praying fervently that the man who had come to her for help would not be killed in front of her eyes.

She was hoping by this time he would have covered himself.

Fortunately the man with her was leading his horse and he could not move as quickly as he wished.

"Why do you want the man you have lost?" Attila asked him.

"That is my business," he replied sharply. "I have to make sure you are not hiding him."

Attila managed to laugh.

"Why should I do so?" she asked. "As I have just told you I am a pupil of Father Jozsef's, who is suffering from a strange illness which the doctors cannot diagnose. That is why we have come to the Shrine and I am sure our prayers will be more effective than their medicine."

"It would not surprise me," the man muttered.

By this time they had reached the carriage.

The sun was sinking and the shadows from the trees made it difficult to see clearly.

Attila pushed herself in front of the man.

She put her right hand on the handle of the door and a finger of her left hand against her lips.

Very quietly she whispered,

"He has been very ill and I cannot allow him to be disturbed."

The man made a grunting noise, but did not speak.

Slowly and softly, so as not to make a noise, Attila opened the door.

As she had hoped it was almost dark inside and it was just possible to see that there was a man in a cassock with a hood over his head lying on the floor of the carriage.

It was impossible to make out his face and the man lent forward and tried to look under the hood.

He could just see a little of his chin and his upper lip.

With a feeling of huge relief Attila realised that he had done as she had told him and removed his moustache.

The leader drew back.

He did not speak and Attila closed the door of the carriage and then, as he realised that she had been right, he mounted his horse.

He rode back to where the other men were waiting for him a little way from the fire.

"He is not here," he said to them. "He must have doubled back into the wood."

One of the men shrugged his shoulders.

"Then it is like looking for a needle in a haystack. If you had not been such a damned fool as to arouse his suspicions, we would have got what we wanted."

He rode off and the others followed him.

They went a short way down the grassland before turning into the wood.

As the last man disappeared Attila gave a deep sigh of relief.

She had won the battle of nerves and they had gone away without finding their victim.

She realised, however, that she must be careful.

If the leader was suspicious, he might be watching them.

Lamos, who had continued his cooking by the fire, looked round.

"Is Your Royal Highness all right," he asked her anxiously.

Attila put her hand to her lips and ran towards him.

"Be careful what you say. I do not wish those men to know who I am, or the man who has just arrived."

"I'm sorry. It just slipped out."

She had told both Lamos and Kilkos not to say who she was when they had been at the Monastery.

"They think I am just a pupil of Father Jozsef's," she said, "and that indeed is the truth."

They had understood that she did not want them to make a great fuss over her.

And now she was sure it would be a great mistake for the stranger, whoever he was, to have any idea she was a Princess.

As if he was upset at having made an error he said,

"I will have something ready for you in about five minutes. Do you expect the stranger will be hungry too?"

"I will go and ask him," replied Attila, "but he will be wise to stay where he is while those men are about."

"I agree with you," said Lamos. "A nasty lot they seemed to me."

Attila went back to the carriage where she looked towards the trees and then opened the door.

"They have gone," she announced.

The stranger sat up and pushed back the hood from his head.

"How can I ever thank you for saving my life? I cannot think of any woman who would have been so quick or so skilful without asking a great number of questions."

Attila smiled.

"In which case they would have caught you."

"And killed me!"

Attila glanced over her shoulder again.

"I think they were convinced you were not here, but one can never be sure. It is very difficult to hide out in the grassland and they think you have returned to the woods."

"It is because you were clever enough to tell me to shave off my moustache that he did believe I was a priest."

"Why does he want to kill you?" enquired Attila.

She thought she must seem rather inquisitive, but at the same time this young man, nice though he seemed, had maybe committed some terrible crime.

"As you have been very kind to me," the stranger answered her, "I am more than prepared to tell you the whole gruesome story. But for the moment I can only feel gratitude that at the very last moment I found an angel to befriend me."

Attila laughed.

"I am delighted that you think of me as an angel, but actually I am only a humble pilgrim."

"And a very beautiful one," he added.

As Attila was not used to being paid compliments, she blushed and then said quickly,

"I am sure you must be feeling hungry and supper, I am told, will be ready in five minutes."

"Will it be safe for me to come out of the carriage?" the stranger asked.

"Only if you wear the cassock and you should keep the hood over your head. If they spy at you from the wood they might recognise you, even though very soon it will be dark."

"You think of everything and I am just so grateful. Is my horse safe?"

She liked it that he was worrying about his horse.

"He is with the other horses down by the stream," she told him. "Ours will come when they are called and I hope yours will do the same."

"He is young but fairly obedient. In fact, he is one of the fastest horses I have ever ridden and there is Arab blood in him."

"Then I must take a look at him," suggested Attila. "I love horses and, if you do too, you will admire mine."

"I am prepared to believe everything about you is perfect!"

Attila blushed again and then she turned away from the carriage.

"Come and join me at the fire if you think it is safe. If they are moving through the woods, we will hear them and you will have time to run back to the carriage."

She did not wait for him to answer but walked over to the fire.

Lamos was already putting what he had cooked into a large china bowl.

Instead of going into the open field, Attila changed her mind. She moved away from the carriage, but kept in the shadows of the trees.

She knew it would be more difficult for anyone to see the stranger if he joined her and as the sun was sinking fast, it would soon be dark.

When she had seated herself, Kilkos spread a small tablecloth over the ground and arranged two plates and two glasses on it.

There were two bottles of Father Jozsef's wine left and Attila told Kilkos to open one of them.

She had only just been seated for a few moments when she saw the stranger coming towards her, wearing Father Jozsef's cassock with the hood firmly over his head.

She considered it would be impossible for anyone watching them to suspect that he was in fact a young man in smart riding clothes.

She noticed that he kept glancing at the wood.

When he joined her, he said,

"We shall hear anyone coming long before they see us."

"That is just what I thought."

"You are so clever I cannot believe you are real, but as you are really an angel from Heaven, I am so very, very grateful to you."

"Because I am hungry I feel, at the moment, very much on earth!"

They both laughed.

The soup Lamos produced was really delicious and the stranger enjoyed Father Jozsef's wine.

"It is different to anything I have ever tasted," he exclaimed.

"That is because Father Jozsef, who you are now impersonating," explained Attila, "added healing herbs and special fruit which makes it not only delicious to drink but heals you if you are ill."

"What has happened to the Father you are speaking about and whose cassock I am wearing?"

There was a little pause before Attila answered him.

"Just when we reached the Shrine he died and was buried this morning."

"I am so sorry," said the stranger quietly. "It must be very upsetting for you."

"I shall miss him more than I can possibly say," she replied. "He was an old man but I know he was happy to go."

"How could you know?"

Again there was a pause while Attila thought what she should say and then somehow it seemed easier to talk to him.

"While he was praying on the mountainside, he saw someone he had loved for many years and who had died."

The words came out slowly yet she felt she had to say them.

"Then he has found what we all seek."

Attila looked at him in surprise.

"Is that what you are seeking?" she enquired.

"Of course. Every man believes in his heart he will find the Golden Fleece or rather the true love which most of us only read about in books and which does not seem to exist in ordinary life."

"But it does, I *know* it does," cried Attila. "Father Jozsef found it and my father found it with my mother."

The stranger smiled.

"That is why you are so beautiful and I have always believed that if two people who are very much in love have a child it is beautiful because their hearts and their souls made it."

Attila stared at him.

"How can you possibly say that? It is something I have often thought, but I have never put it into words."

"Now I think of it, it is something I have never said before," said the stranger. "But because you saved my life you realise you are now responsible for me. You must be aware that is one of the oldest legends in existence."

Attila chuckled.

"It is a rather frightening one, but I have read that is what some people believe."

"Well, I believe it and thus I am at your service and of course you have taken on a very big responsibility!"

He was joking and yet Attila felt there was some truth behind what he was saying.

"Now you are making me feel apprehensive, but at the same time I am very, very glad I was able to save you."

"With an unbelievable brilliance! No other woman would have thought so quickly or found the right answer to such a dangerous situation?"

"Would those men really have killed you?"

"It was because I found out what they were trying to do that I ran away," answered the stranger.

"Unless it upsets you, I am of course very curious to know what happened."

"Then I will tell you. The man who came to look at

me is my cousin. He wants me dead so that he can inherit what I possess and take my place in the family."

"And he is prepared to kill you to do so?" asked Attila, thinking it was incredible.

"He thought out a very clever plot. I have this new horse of which I am very proud. He told me he had found a jump on my land which he thought would make a perfect challenge in the race we usually arrange every year. It is an occasion which has been handed down for generations."

"So you took your horse to the jump."

"I went riding with the other men you saw just now who are all friends of my cousin. I had a look at the jumps and my cousin had improved them considerably since last year. He had raised them and he had also made some new jumps which I had not seen previously."

Attila was listening wide-eyed.

More food was provided by Lamos while they were talking, but Attila was so interested that she ate it without really tasting what she was putting into her mouth.

"I took my horse, which is called Zeus, over two of the jumps and then as if I was being prompted by someone unseen, I rode to look at the last jump before I took Zeus over it."

"And what did you see?" enquired Attila.

"As I was looking at the jump, I realised that one of my cousin's friends was on the other side of it and the way he was holding something under his arm made me feel suspicious."

"What was he holding?"

"I suspected, and I was right, that what he intended to do was to shoot at my horse when we took the jump. He would fall bringing me with him and if I was not dead after I had fallen, I would certainly have been suffocated before I was taken back to the house."

"I cannot believe it!" exclaimed Attila breathlessly.

"I found it hard to believe myself, but I realised the only thing I could do was to run away."

He drew in his breath as if he was remembering how frightened he had been as he resumed his story.

"Before they realised what had happened I galloped as fast as I could away from the jumps and into the woods. When I heard them following me I knew that if they caught me, I would not go home alive."

"I have never heard anything so horrible, so beastly and so cruel," cried Attila.

"When men are greedy – they will stop at nothing," the stranger told her philosophically.

"But if you go back, will he not try again?"

"My cousin may try, but now I am so alerted to his devilry, I am certain that when I do return, he will realise that it would be a mistake for us ever to meet again."

"You cannot be too sure that he will feel like that."

"I will make certain, but now I am forewarned and thanks to you I am still alive."

"I am frightened by what you have experienced," murmured Attila. "And if he does try again, he might be successful."

"Then, as I am now your responsibility," he said, "you will have to protect me."

He was speaking lightly.

But his blue eyes gave Attila a most strange feeling in her breasts that she had never known before.

She only knew, although it seemed incredible, that she wanted to protect this man.

Even though she did not know his name!

CHAPTER FIVE

Attila awoke because she heard the man next to her moving about.

She guessed that Kilkos was bringing him some hot water for shaving, as he had always done for Father Jozsef.

Now she thought it all over, the terror of last night seemed so unbelievable and it was as if it just could not have happened.

Could it really be possible those men would have killed the man who had come to her for help?

It did not seem credible and yet the way he spoke had been so sincere she did not doubt it.

She dressed quickly, thinking it would be a good idea if they moved on, well away from the woods where so much danger lurked.

She walked to the place where they had eaten the night before and two minutes later the stranger joined her.

He was wearing Father Jozsef's cassock over his riding clothes, which Attila now could see were very smart.

As she looked at him in the daylight she realised he was extremely handsome.

He sat down beside her.

"Good morning, my protecting angel," he began. "I am hoping I can at least eat my breakfast before we start being frightened again!"

"I was indeed terrified last night," sighed Attila.

"And so was I," replied the stranger.

Lamos had cooked appetising eggs and bacon for breakfast and there was toast and honey as well excellent hot coffee with fresh cream.

The sun was shining and the world around them was so beautiful and serene.

Attila felt happy and for the moment unafraid.

They were drinking coffee when the stranger said,

"I think that now it is the time for us to introduce ourselves. My name is Gesa."

It was an unusual name, but Attila recognised that it was Hungarian and she thought perhaps, because he rode so well, he came from that country.

"I am now waiting to hear your name," he added, as Attila had apparently forgotten to answer him.

She had already made up her mind during the night that it would be a mistake for her to tell him her name was Attila.

He would know she came from Valdina by the way she spoke.

Her mother had always called her 'Lala' as it was what she had called herself when she was a small child.

She therefore replied,

"My name is Lala and I am delighted to meet you, Gesa."

"I should rise up and bow, but instead allow me to kiss your hand."

He bent forward and picked up her hand.

He raised it to his lips, which briefly touched her skin.

Attila felt the same strange quiver run through her body as last night.

Because once again she felt shy, she said quickly,

"I think we should move off as quickly as possible. These horrible men might come back and continue looking for you."

"You are right, Lala, and I therefore intend to travel inside your carriage until we are far away from here."

He gave a laugh before he added,

"It has been altered in a very clever way to make an apartment for two people."

"I thought that myself and it was very fortunate that Father Jozsef's cassock was there when you needed it."

"I have sent a prayer up to him in Heaven and I also sent one to you."

"Let us hope we are as lucky today as yesterday."

She rose as she spoke and they carried their plates, cups and saucers back to Lamos.

It was then as Attila saw Kilkos saddling her horse that she had an idea.

"If the men who are looking for you and see your horse, they will undoubtedly recognise it, even if you are riding in a cassock."

Gesa stared at her.

"You are right! Of course you are right! But what can I do about it?"

"What I suggest," Attila began slowly as if she was thinking it out, "is that I will ride your horse and Kilkos will then ride mine. He will lead the third horse which was Father Jozsef's and that is the one your enemies will be looking at."

"You are very astute, Lala, I should have thought of that myself."

Kilkos who had been listening picked up the saddle which belonged to Gesa and hid it away.

Then as Gesa disappeared into the carriage, Attila mounted his horse.

She realised it was an exceptional stallion and one of the finest horses she had ever ridden.

She hoped that her father would have a chance of seeing it and then she remembered that Gesa did not know who she was.

Before they arrived in Valdina she would have to explain to him that she was going to the Palace.

Then she thought this idea might end in trouble and perhaps it would be best to say goodbye when they were on the outskirts of Valdina.

She settled herself in the saddle and picked up her reins and as she did so she became aware that Lamos was standing on the top of the driving seat, looking ahead.

He could obviously see very much further than she could on the ground.

As they waited Attila asked,

"Can you see anything? Is there any sign of those men?"

"I thought, although I might have been mistaken," replied Lamos, "that I saw one slip into the wood about a mile further on."

"Then we must be extremely careful and it would be wise for me not to ride too far ahead of you."

She spoke quietly, but at the same time her heart was beating and again she was feeling afraid.

Would those dastardly men watching out for Gesa actually pull him out of the carriage?

Would they kill him without giving him a chance to defend himself?

Or would they just carry him away to the wood and she would never hear of him again.

These troublesome thoughts all passed through her mind like streaks of lightning, but she recognised there was nothing she could do about it.

If they turned round and went back, they would still have to undertake the journey tomorrow.

It would not be possible to take the carriage through the thick grassland or to approach Valdina from any other direction.

'I shall have to pray really hard that Father Jozsef will protect us,' Attila told herself.

Lamos was in his seat and was moving the horses forward and having had a restful night and plenty to eat, they were only too eager to move quickly.

Zeus wanted to gallop and Attila had to hold him in to prevent him rushing off long before the rest of the party.

It seemed to take a long time before the two horses pulling the carriage had passed by the wood where Lamos thought he had seen one of the assailants.

Attila realised that she must not stare and yet she kept glancing upwards as she rode past the trees.

She expected to see behind each one the men who had pursued Gesa last night.

They must have travelled for nearly a mile.

Then she was aware there was a horseman hidden behind the next trees they were about to pass.

She pulled in Zeus.

They were in more or less a group as they reached the danger point and the man in the trees would only have a quick glimpse of her.

She hoped he would not be interested in the horse she rode and that his eyes would go to where, half-hidden by the carriage, Kilkos was riding Attila's horse.

They travelled on further without any interruption and Attila knew that their subterfuge had been successful.

Nevertheless her heart was beating so tumultuously that she was finding it difficult to breathe.

Only when they had quickened their pace and were half a mile away from the danger point did she sigh with relief.

Now she could breathe more steadily and her heart was no longer turning somersaults.

It would have been foolhardy to stop so they carried on for nearly an hour and then they found a place where there were no trees and nowhere anyone could hide except on the mountains themselves.

Lamos drew in his horses and Attila turned round and rode back to the carriage.

"Why are you stopping?" she asked.

"I think that the gentleman has had enough rough and tumble inside the carriage and if he wants to get out he is safe enough just here. We could see anyone approaching when they were over a mile away."

Attila agreed with him and Gesa must have heard what Lamos was saying as he opened the carriage door and stepped out.

"I feel as if I have been swimming in a rough sea," he said. "But thank you all the same, I am very grateful."

"You will be all right now, sir," said Lamos. "But better we move on as we've still a long way to go."

"I know and I am looking forward to riding Zeus."

He looked at Attila as he spoke and she laughed.

"I was a little afraid you would want him to have him back. He is a magnificent horse and I am not surprised you are very proud of him."

"I think actually," said Gesa, as he helped her down

from the saddle, "I would have minded Zeus having to die last night more than dying myself."

"You are not to talk about it, Gesa. It all still scares me and the sooner we reach home and safety, the better."

Gesa was busy undoing the girths of the side saddle on Zeus's back and as he lifted it off, Attila asked him,

"I had not thought of it before, but will it be safe for you to go home."

"I shall be more than safe once I have returned to my own home. It was only that I was foolish enough to go to the racecourse with my cousin a long distance away."

He put the saddle down on the ground and Kilkos came towards him with his own saddle.

It was difficult to talk privately while the two men were attending to the horses and so Attila waited until she and Gesa were riding side by side.

They galloped on until they were well ahead of the carriage and Attila could ask him the question which was troubling her.

"Are you certain that your wicked cousin will not be waiting for you when you do return home?"

"I promise I will deal with him before he has any chance of threatening me again. Now I have realised how dangerous he is, I will not take any chances."

"Where do you live, Gesa?"

There was a silence before he replied and she knew instinctively he was not going to tell her the truth.

"What I want to talk about at the moment," he said, "is *you*. We have had my disreputable cousin upsetting us twice and quite frankly I find your conversation far more interesting than his."

"I am not surprised!" exclaimed Attila, recognising that he had avoided answering her question.

At the same time she wanted to talk to Gesa about a thousand different subjects, all far more interesting than the horror and fear his enemies had engendered.

She smiled at him as they were driving through the thick grassland with the butterflies moving ahead of them in clouds of fluttering yellow.

"I realise that you are being evasive, Gesa, but I am curious as to where you come from and what you do."

"I might say the same about you, Lala, except I am quite certain you have just dropped down from Heaven to help me and it is not possible for me to join you up there!"

"You cannot be too certain of it. At the same time it is exciting for me to make a new acquaintance."

Gesa raised his eyebrows.

"Exciting? Surely looking as you do you can have little difficulty in meeting new people, especially men and you must get bored listening to their compliments."

Attila gave a giggle.

"I wish it was true, but I do live a very quiet and secluded life and, although you may not believe it, I see very few people of my own age."

"I find that hard to believe, but as I think our ages are quite near each other, if I am somewhat of a novelty, so please tell me why."

"It is difficult to put into words what I think about you, Gesa. Perhaps because I have met so few young men, I am more used to having older men talk while I listen."

Gesa laughed.

"Of course they do and it is what they do to me. Quite frankly I find it exceedingly annoying."

"It is a good way to learn, but equally it is rather a question of all work and no play!"

"Of course it is," agreed Gesa. "That is why you and I must play and laugh while we do it."

Without meaning to Attila looked apprehensively over her shoulder.

She was half afraid they were challenging the Gods and at any moment fear and danger would be back again.

"Forget them!" said Gesa, reading her thoughts. "I promise they will not follow us any further."

"How can you be so sure?"

"Because once out of their own territory they have no power and I think no one would ever trust them as I was stupid enough to do."

"You must be very careful in the future, Gesa."

"Would it matter to you if I was not?"

Attila could not quite think how she should answer that question.

Then as she looked at him, their eyes met.

Somehow everything around them disappeared and she could only see him and it was as if he felt the same and could not look away.

Then his horse stumbled and he had to pull in the reins.

"Is it not time for luncheon," he enquired. "I want to talk to you."

"I think there is a place ahead where we stopped on the way and I expect Lamos intends to go there again."

She was quite right.

Lamos drove the carriage into the shade of some rocks and Kilkos took his horse and the one he was leading down to the river.

"Let us have our luncheon by the river," suggested Gesa. "It will be cooler there and I cannot allow the sun to spoil the beauty of your skin."

Attila laughed.

"No one has ever worried about my skin before."

"I can only imagine the men in Valdina are blind as well as deaf!"

She looked at him enquiringly.

"Your voice is exquisite and just like music," he explained, "and your skin has the beauty and softness of lilies."

Attila blushed and turned her head away, but she was feeling how exciting it was to be paid such extravagant compliments which she had never heard before.

There was a place by the water where they were in the shade and also out of sight of the carriage.

Lamos had prepared a cold luncheon for them and yet it looked very appetising when it was all laid out on the tablecloth.

There were two bottles of wine, one being Father Jozsef's speciality and the other came from the Monastery.

Gesa made Attila try a little of both and she much preferred Father Jozsef's.

She was, however, not very interested in what she was drinking and she really had no idea what she ate.

She was fascinated by everything Gesa was telling her and she listened wide-eyed while he described a visit he had made recently to Russia and another to France.

"I came to know the people quite well," he related. "Not only those I was staying with, but the ordinary people of both countries. They taught me so much and they had a fascination for life which I believe is vital for everyone to have wherever they live."

"Fascinating in what sort of way," enquired Attila.

"Not only in their looks and the way they live, but

what they thought, and it is something very important in this day and age when so much is happening in our lives to know what people think and why they think it."

Attila knew what he was trying to say and because it amused her, she started to question him about the way he used his mind.

If he thought in a different way, she said he might be of greater significance to his country and the people he lived with.

It was the sort of conversation she would have had with her father when he was well and it was always very exciting to criticise, to agree and to criticise again.

Especially with this handsome young man.

She soon realised he was most intelligent and well-read.

"How do you know so much about the world," she asked him. "When you have obviously only visited a small part of it."

"I have read a great deal," he replied, "and I have cultivated men and women from other countries when I get a chance to meet them. Last year I met a man from Egypt who told me so much I did not know. About the Pyramids, the Sphinx and the philosophy that lies behind them."

Attila gave a little cry.

"That is what I would like to know. Oh, please tell me what you have learnt."

Gesa looked up at the sky.

"It is what I would really like to do, but at the same time I think we should be moving on. You have another night to spend before you reach home."

It was with difficulty that Attila did not say she was glad about that.

Now there was no more danger she wanted to stay

with Gesa, as she felt he was telling her so much she had never known.

Equally he was giving her something else which she could not put into words.

*

They rode a long way in the next few hours.

Sometimes they were racing against each other and sometimes they let their horses walk at a slow pace through the grass while they talked.

Finally Kilkos brought the carriage to an abrupt halt and Attila became aware that if they carried on for another two hours they could reach Valdina.

She had no wish to hurry on and she found herself dreading the moment she would be back in the Palace.

She would have to explain where she had been to her stepmother, who she knew would be really furious at her leaving before Prince Otto arrived.

She might even have him still waiting for her or she might have found another man she wanted her to marry.

Attila's heart sank at the mere thought of it.

It would be difficult to obtain her father's support without upsetting him.

Worst of all would be the horror of being married to a man she did not know or love.

But tonight she would have Gesa to talk to and she asked for nothing more.

They had dinner together in a secluded spot and sat talking until the stars came out over their heads and the moon shone down on them turning Attila's hair to silver.

Gesa told her again and again how lovely she was.

"You are not to embarrass me," she told him. "I am unused to compliments and although I do not believe them, I find them rather embarrassing."

"Why should you not believe them, Lala? I swear that everything I say to you is the truth and nothing but the truth."

"Then you must have met very few women, Gesa. I am always being told how beautiful the Russian women are and the French are reckoned to be the most fascinating in the whole world."

"But you have something *different*."

"What is that?" asked Attila.

"It is difficult to put into words, but I believe that your beauty is not only skin deep, but comes from your heart and soul, which make it shine out overwhelmingly and I am certain that once a man has looked at you, it is impossible for him to look away."

Attila drew in her breath.

"That is something I would really like to believe," she murmured, "but I suspect because you express it so movingly, you have said it already to quite a number of women!"

"Now you are insulting me," replied Gesa, "I have told you the truth. I find you so lovely not only in your looks but in your thoughts that I feel like picking you up in my arms and riding away with you, so that you will never see anyone but me again."

The way he spoke sounded completely sincere.

Attila did not know how to answer him and Gesa moved a little nearer to her.

"Now I want you to answer a question truthfully," he said.

"I am always truthful."

"I am sure that is true and it is another fantastic and unusual thing about you."

"And what is your question, Gesa?"

He looked deeply into her eyes which seemed to have caught the light from the stars.

"Have you ever been kissed?"

"No, of course not," Attila replied quickly.

"Why do you say 'of course not'."

"Because I would not want anyone to try to kiss me unless I loved him and I have never loved anyone."

"Are you sure of that?" enquired Gesa.

She became very conscious that now he was almost touching her.

She once again felt a strange excitement coursing through her and she still could not explain it.

"I think, my lovely angel, that at the moment we are in a world of our own and there is no one to disturb us. We are, in fact, one with the stars and the moon."

Attila put back her head and looked up at the sky.

As she did so, Gesa pulled her against him and his lips were on hers.

She could not believe what was happening.

Then as she felt a thrill run through her entire being he drew her closer still.

His lips became more possessive, more demanding.

Attila had often wondered what it would be like to be kissed.

Now she knew it was beyond anything she could ever have imagined or anything she had dreamed about.

It was wonderful! Marvellous! Glorious!

At the same time it was *magical.*

As Gesa kept on kissing her, she felt as if he carried her up into the stars.

They were no longer human beings on earth but one with the angels.

His kisses were not human but spiritual.

It was a long time before Gesa raised his head.

"*I love you*, my darling Lala," he sighed, "as I have never thought it possible to love anyone."

"*You love me*?" Attila whispered.

"I do love you," Gesa replied firmly. "Now tell me what you are feeling?"

"It is so marvellous, there are no words to express it. I think perhaps we have died and were not aware of it!"

Gesa gave a little laugh.

"We are not dead, my lovely one, but very much alive. I have now found you when I thought it would be impossible and what I wanted was merely a figment of my imagination."

"What do you mean?" asked Attila.

"It is *you*. I could not believe that you existed. I thought that all my life I should be alone, because what I yearned for was not only out of reach but did not exist."

He paused for a moment.

"Now I have found you and you are mine. I will kill any man who tries to take you away from me!"

He did not wait for her to answer, but was kissing her once again, kissing her with possessive and passionate kisses which made her whole body tremble.

It was ecstasy so intense it was almost painful.

Only as he stopped kissing Attila, because he was breathless, did she say,

"I love you, *I love you*, Gesa, I did not know it was possible to feel like this. Oh, Gesa I have prayed for love and now God has given it to me."

"He has given you to me," he murmured, "and no one shall ever take you from me."

Then he was kissing her again and there was no need for words.

They had both in their minds, their hearts and their souls found the love they had sought for so long.

*

It was after midnight before Gesa would let Attila go back to the carriage.

When they reached it there was no sign of the two men in charge, but she knew they would be asleep under the carriage.

The horses were lying near them quite content and comfortable in the long grass.

Gesa took Attila over to the carriage and opened the door for her.

"It is an agony to leave you, my darling," he said, "but when we are married, you will sleep in my arms and we will be together by day and by night."

"*When we are married*?" Attila stammered.

"Can we do anything else? You are mine and I am yours. How could we ever contemplate being married to anyone else?"

He did not wait for an answer but kissed her again.

He kissed her until it was impossible for Attila to think and she could only quiver with the excitement and wonder of his lips.

He kissed her eyes and her forehead and then he forced himself to leave her.

He walked round the carriage to climb in on his own side.

Attila undressed.

Her whole being was singing with the wonder of love. It was quite impossible to think or speculate about tomorrow.

After sleeping for a while she awoke.

She was acutely aware that Gesa was near her, but they were firmly divided by a strong wooden board and she wondered if he too was awake and thinking about her.

Then the full wonder of what she had felt when he kissed her swept over her again.

'*I love him*, I adore him,' she whispered to herself.

Because she could not prevent it a question forced itself through her happiness.

Would she be allowed to marry him?

She had no knowledge of who he was.

He had not even told her his other name.

She could imagine what her stepmother would say about him.

More importantly Attila knew that her father would question the possibility of her marrying a commoner.

If she was married to anyone who was not Royal, it might be impossible for her to become Queen of Valdina on her father's death.

She would still be the person of most importance in the country and a consort who would share her life would have to be accepted by the people.

She knew without being told he would have to be of some considerable influence himself.

Anyone they thought was an ordinary man and did not come from an aristocratic family would be sent away without her even being consulted about him.

All through history the dynasty of Valdina had been of great significance and its Ruler held his place amongst Royalty in other parts of the world.

It had not been easy as Valdina was a small country compared with Hungary or any of their other neighbours.

Yet because they were definitely Royal, there had never been any question of them not being acknowledged by all the other Kings and Princes of the region.

Prince Otto was a man of disrepute and dear Father Jozsef and everyone else spoke of him disparagingly.

Yet he was Royal and also the Ruler of quite a large Principality.

In her anxiety to be rid of her, Attila knew that her stepmother had chosen cleverly.

However much the King's advisers disliked Prince Otto, they would find it hard to refute him altogether.

Attila shivered.

Supposing they contemplated accepting Prince Otto on her behalf, how could she possibly propose Gesa taking his place?

Perhaps he had nothing more to commend him than his looks, his brain and his superb horse.

'He must have some other advantages,' she thought desperately.

It all boiled down to the fact that if his blood was not Royal, he would not be accepted by Valdina.

It was with difficulty she did not get out of bed, go round the carriage and beg him to reassure her.

If the truth was even worse than she feared, it was too agonising to face.

'How can I live without him now that I have found him? And could anyone else make me feel as I feel now?'

She knew without being told it was impossible.

She had prayed at the Shrine of Love and now she had found the love that Father Jozsef had told her one day would be hers.

Yet having found it she would have to lose it.

She thought rather than lose him that she would run away with Gesa.

The question was – would he take her?

He might harbour no wish to take for his wife a Princess who was no longer Royal and who was despised by her countrymen because she put her own desires before duty.

Therefore she had no place in her own country.

Would he think it did not matter?

Would he mind?

Would he believe that love was more important than anything else?

Would he perhaps take her away to some obscure island where no one would ever find them again?

Attila knew that this was just impossible.

No young man could sacrifice his whole life to a woman and give up everything else.

His hunting, his shooting, his riding!

The games with men of his own age and most of all his friends.

However much he loved a woman, Attila was wise enough to know a man needed the company of his own sex and he must also pit their brains against other men.

'If I took him away from all of that, he would soon begin to hate me,' she told herself. 'Then we would have nothing between us, not even our hearts.'

She wanted to cry out at the agony in her heart.

Yet she kept thinking that tomorrow, if only for a little while, she would still be with him.

Perhaps he would kiss her again as he had kissed her tonight and she would feel the glory of his love seeping through her body.

Once again he would be carrying her up to the stars.

'I love him, I adore him,' she said to herself over and over again.

Yet there was a little devil sitting on her shoulder, whispering into her ear that it was all a dream and when she awoke, she would come back to reality.

Then there would be nothing but the ashes of a fire which had burned out.

Attila covered her eyes with her hands, knowing that now she was past praying.

Past asking God to let her live with the illusion that everything could be perfect and she could marry Gesa.

In fact they would have perhaps three or four hours together and then that would be the end.

He would be sent away and she would watch him go, knowing he had taken her heart with him.

Once again the thought flashed through her mind that the only thing she could do was to tell him the truth.

She would suggest they might elope, but her father would be furious.

He might even have Gesa arrested and the marriage annulled.

She would then be forced back to the Palace and instead of it being the home she loved, it would be a prison from which she could not escape.

"Duty! Duty! Duty!"

She could hear the Ministers saying it to her over and over again.

"It is your duty to Valdina."

"It is your duty to your people."

"It is your duty to your family."

"It is your duty to your Royal blood."

There was no way out.

There was no escape.

She could see it as if it was a map laid out in front of her and for the rest of her life once Gesa had left her, she could only dream of him.

Having lost him, she would have lost everything that ever mattered in life itself.

"I love him! *I love him*!" she cried in her heart.

The tears ran down her cheeks.

CHAPTER SIX

The morning that Attila had left the Palace the King deliberately did not ring the bell for his valet until eleven o'clock.

When Frederik came to call him, he pulled back the curtains and the King said,

"Frederik, I need your help."

He knew that the man who had been with him for many years was always delighted if he was taken into his confidence.

"You know I will do anything Your Majesty does require," replied Frederik as he stood by the bed.

"My daughter, Her Royal Highness, was talking to me last night and she said it was a mistake for me to take this medicine which is doing me no good and the sleeping draught which always leaves me muzzy in the morning. I have now decided to stop them."

"That is good news, Your Majesty. I never thought them doctors were any good, but it weren't my business to say so."

"I am your business, Frederik. Now what I want you to do is to throw away what they have given me, but without them or Her Majesty being aware of it."

He saw a faint smile on his valet's lips and he knew he disliked the Queen, but Frederik had, of course, been too well-trained to say so.

He could sense Frederik stiffening as Queen Margit came into the room.

"I will pretend I am taking it," the King carried on, "but I am hoping with the water from Salem, I shall soon be feeling so much better."

"The water has just now arrived, Your Majesty, so would Your Majesty like the bath hot or cold?"

The King thought for a moment.

"I think cold, Frederik. Has the food arrived too?"

"The chef has asked me to tell Your Majesty that the eggs for breakfast are from Salem and he be preparing the other food for luncheon."

The King smiled as that at any rate had passed by without any trouble and he was certain that what Father Jozsef had told him would come true.

He had a cold bath and he was reciting as he did so what Attila had told him to say to himself.

'I am getting well! I am getting well!'

It was after midday when the Queen visited him.

"I am rather worried, Sigismund," she said, as she came to his bedside. "There is no sign of Attila anywhere and I cannot think where she can be."

"She is quite all right," the King replied. "I thought I told you she was going to stay with friends."

"You have told me nothing of the sort," she retorted sharply. "What friends and why?"

"She said they had asked her to go for a few days and I thought it would be good for her to get away. After all now I am in bed she misses our rides together."

"If you ask me," the Queen said angrily, "Attila has deliberately gone away so as to avoid the party I am giving for Prince Otto."

"I think that party will be a mistake," said the King. "I have heard some unpleasant things about the Prince and he is not someone I particularly welcome to the Palace."

The Queen made a sound which he knew was one of indignation and then with an effort she controlled herself saying,

"It is very unlike you, dearest, to be so prejudiced. I found Prince Otto a charming young man and I am sure when she meets him Attila will like him very much."

"Well, she is not here at present, so that question will not arise."

"Wherever she is," the Queen said quickly, "I must insist on her returning immediately. I have gone to a great deal of trouble over this party and it is absolutely absurd for her to miss it."

The King always recognised that when his wife's voice rose, it meant that she was losing her temper and the ensuing argument between them, apart from anything else, would be undignified.

He closed his eyes and said in a weak voice,

"I am too tired to think about it now. I must go to sleep."

He was aware without being able to see her that the Queen hesitated.

She wanted to force him to make a decision and yet as he lay with his eyes closed without speaking, she knew it would be wrong to arouse him.

After a moment she stalked out of the bedroom and with some difficulty closed the door quietly behind her.

The King opened his eyes, appreciating that by this time Attila would be a long way from the Palace.

Even if the Queen was so unwise as to send some of the guards to look for her, they would not find her.

The King thought it was very kind of Father Jozsef and Attila to make such a long journey on his behalf.

He had heard of the miracles created by St. Janos

and he desperately wanted their prayers to be answered and he could be himself again.

It seemed impossible that the water and the food from Salem could do much for him and yet Father Jozsef would not tell him a lie, not even to make him happy.

He had assured him that the people of Salem were in much better health than anyone else, so there must be something in their water and land which did not exist in Valdina.

The King thought later that night and again the next day that he really did feel a little better.

Yet he was sensible enough to think it was too soon to be optimistic.

*

On the third day after Attila's departure he was able to say to Frederik,

"The pain in my chest is much better. I am finding it easier to breath and I am feeling much more energetic."

"If you ask me, Your Majesty, you are on the right road to recovery and Her Royal Highness will be jumping for joy when she gets back."

The King knew that this was true and a day later he could say quite honestly he felt very much better.

He talked to Frederik about getting up.

"The doctors are asking if they can come and see Your Majesty," Frederik told him.

"Oh no!" he exclaimed. "I don't want them."

"That is what I think and I told them Your Majesty was taking things easy, but was feeling a bit better. It'd be a mistake to disturb you."

"You are quite right, Frederik, the last thing I want is to have them croaking over me and making examinations for which there is no answer!"

He bathed in the water from Salem twice a day and drank a great deal of it.

He also found the food which the chef cooked was more delicious than anything he had eaten previously.

The King sent for the Senior Chef, who told him he was delighted with the quality of everything he received from Salem.

In fact, although he paid what they asked, it was cheaper than the prices they had been paying in the City.

The King was aware every night when the Queen came to say goodnight to him that she glanced at an inlaid chest he was using as a dressing table.

She was looking, he knew, to see if his sleeping draught was ready for him.

Frederik always put it on a silver tray with a glass of water, but now he threw it away every morning.

The King had not really been well enough to climb out of bed unnecessarily, but now he was so much better he was able to walk jauntily in his own particular way to his bath.

He would also stand looking out of the window at the garden before he went back to bed.

But this evening when he had had his bath, he said to Frederik,

"I am going to get up tomorrow."

"Now don't be in a hurry," Frederik said rather like a fussy Nanny. "Your Majesty be getting better, but slow, slow be better than quick – quick – then crash!"

"I am well aware of that, but at the same time I do feel very different! Whether it is the magic water or the delicious food from Salem, I am surely being transformed from a dying man into one who intends to live!"

"Of course Your Majesty will live! What would Her

Royal Highness do I'd like to know? She wouldn't be happy in the Palace, that's for sure!"

The King was more than aware that the Queen did not like her stepdaughter and Attila, although she tried to hide it, disliked the Queen.

'Women! Women!' the King moaned to himself.

Equally he now realised that he had made a mistake in marrying again.

He had been so desperately unhappy when he lost the wife he adored and he could not bear to be alone.

Attila was too young to take her mother's place and as she was working very hard with her tutors she had to go to bed early.

She rode with him in the morning and had luncheon with him, but she was still of an age when it was thought she was too young to come down to dinner.

This meant the King had to dine alone or he must invite a courtier or Minister to join him and on the whole he found them boring as he preferred female company.

He and Queen Anna had always looked forward to the evenings when the work of the day was over and they could be alone together.

They liked to dine in their private sitting room and laugh at each other's jokes.

Then as they wanted to be closer still they would walk with their arms around each other to their bedroom.

It had been an almost unbearable agony at night for the King to sleep alone, knowing that never again would his wife's soft warm body be close to his.

Princess Margit had been a friend for some time.

She came from a small Principality which had little to recommend it except they occasionally bred some rather fine horses.

She was over thirty and she made up her mind that she would find herself another husband, who would be of far greater standing than her father and the Prince she had earlier married in a marriage of convenience.

The Prince ruled a small Principality adjoining the one in which Margit was born. He was getting on in years, but he wanted an heir above all else.

Princess Margit had not been asked if she wished to marry the Prince and found herself his wife almost before she had time to think about it.

He really meant to be kind, but he was a rough and somewhat unpleasant man and she was beginning to dislike him even before their honeymoon was over.

What was worse an heir to the Principality did not appear.

The Princess was certain it was not her fault and the Prince blamed her not himself.

When he had a heart attack and died, she was very delighted and free to return to her home and her father.

She was, however, determined to marry again and this time she would choose the bridegroom herself.

She had, of course, met King Sigismund of Valdina many times.

She found him a most handsome and attractive man and when he lost his wife she realised this was her great opportunity.

She managed to arrange an invitation to stay in the Palace and she told the King how sorry she was for Attila.

Her father wished to give him a very special horse as a present.

The King accepted the horse, but when it arrived, Princess Margit came with it.

She had somehow succeeded in extending her stay

in the Palace for far longer than anyone expected and made the very best of it.

When she dined alone with the King, she made him laugh and he had not laughed since his wife died.

She rode with him and took a great interest in his garden and only when he was present did she make a great fuss of Attila.

The King could not remember later whether he had asked Margit to marry him or she had asked him.

Somehow it seemed at the time the one thing which would make him just a little less miserable and he therefore agreed they should be married.

Actually because he was not so much alone, his life did appear to improve a little, but he was soon aware that Margit intended to have her own way.

It was easier to give in to her than to argue and if there was one thing the King disliked, it was people who argued.

Especially when they were women.

It was not long before he was admitting to himself that he had made a mistake.

Being alone was better for him than to hear Queen Margit's voice rising almost to a shriek as she argued and argued over everything large or small which did not please her.

Fortunately Attila was still not old enough to spend any more time with her father.

She had finished with her teachers and could ride with him in the morning and unless he had some particular duty at which ladies were excluded, she would accompany him wherever he had to go.

Unfortunately if it was anything really spectacular the Queen insisted on coming too.

The King was intelligent enough to realise that as soon as he was ill, the Queen was plotting to take his place if he died.

He was determined that Attila should rule Valdina on his death and he wanted to make certain that she took his place without any outward hostility.

He had spoken only a few days earlier to the Prime Minister.

"I am sure Your Majesty is not going to die," the Prime Minister said, "but if such an unfortunate occurrence for Valdina did happen, I promise I would suggest that Her Royal Highness Attila should take your Majesty's place."

"I have a feeling that there might be a great deal of opposition," he responded. "As you know my daughter is still very young and the Queen is, I think, determined that she should be accepted as my successor."

The King paused for a moment before he added,

"It was indeed her great-grandmother who ruled her own Principality and was in fact most successful."

"So I have heard," replied the Prime Minister, "but as Your Majesty is exceedingly popular with your subjects, I am sure they would much prefer to have the Princess on the throne rather than Her Majesty the Queen. Although it might of course be somewhat difficult."

The King was only too conscious of the difficulties and who would make them.

He lay awake wondering what he could do about it, but as he felt so very much better now the question would not arise and if the Queen was very disappointed she could hardly say so.

He had learned from one of his *aides-de-camp* that the Queen was taking a great deal of unexpected interest in the business of the Principality.

"Her Majesty has asked to be present at the meeting of the Cabinet," the *aide-de-camp* informed him.

The King stiffened.

It had been a tradition that once a week the Cabinet would meet in the Palace as it saved the King travelling to the Houses of Parliament.

And it gave him an opportunity to discuss more private matters.

"Has the Prime Minister agreed to her request?" the King asked.

The *aide-de-camp* looked over his shoulder as if he thought someone might be listening.

Reassured, he said in a low voice,

"The Prime Minister agreed to Her Majesty being present at some meetings but not all."

He paused and the King demanded,

"Then what have you done about it?"

"Well, Her Majesty insists she has to know what is going on and she has arranged a listening post behind the bookcase at the far end of the Throne Room in which, as Your Majesty knows, the Privy Council and the Cabinet always meet."

"*Listening post*!" he exclaimed in astonishment.

"Yes, Your Majesty, that is why I thought I should tell Your Majesty."

"I would have been annoyed if you had not told me."

"It has been very cleverly done," the *aide-de-camp* explained, "and of course none of the Cabinet or the Prime Minister has the least idea that what they are debating is being overheard."

The King thought it was outrageous, but it was not something he could say to the *aide-de-camp*.

He appreciated one point all too clearly, that if he died his daughter would have a very difficult battle if she was to take his place as was her destiny.

It worried him and yet he had been feeling too ill to do anything about it.

Now that he was feeling better there was one action he must do at once and that was to make quite certain when the meetings of the Cabinet took place at the Palace there was no chance of there being any eavesdroppers.

Equally he felt the whole scenario was becoming a bit unpleasant and it must not be allowed to continue.

'I will now get really well,' he determined, 'and it is always the same, if you are not on your guard, people will behave in an outrageous manner.'

However, he could not think of anyone who was behaving in an outrageous manner except for the Queen.

It was an issue he could not discuss with her, not only because he disliked a scene of any sort, but he knew she would be very suspicious as to who had told him.

In consequence everyone at the Palace would suffer whether they were innocent or guilty.

'I must get well. I must get well,' the King was saying over and over to himself when the Queen came in to say goodnight.

The party for Prince Otto had taken place on the previous evening and the Queen had told him that it had been a great success and it was such a great pity he had not been present.

"You would have enjoyed it, Sigismund, and when we danced afterwards I thought how delightful it would be if I was waltzing with you."

"I hope the Prince proved a suitable substitute," the King replied, trying to keep the sarcasm out of his voice.

"He was delighted. He admired the Palace and said how sorry he was you were not well enough to receive him."

The King had talked in confidence earlier to one of his older courtiers who had been present. He had been a friend of his for a great many years.

"What was young Otto like?" he enquired. "I have heard some very unpleasant reports about him."

"I am quite certain, Your Majesty, they were not at all exaggerated."

The King raised his eyebrows.

"As bad as that?"

"Worse! He is the type of young man I would not allow any of my daughters to meet and I am only thankful that Princess Attila was staying away with her friends."

"What you are really saying," said the King, "is that Prince Otto should not have been a guest in my Palace."

The old courtier laughed.

"You are putting extra words into my mouth, Your Majesty, but I am not denying them!"

He then told the King several stories about Prince Otto, which did not exactly shake him, but they did make him believe that it was a grave mistake for the Prince to have been a visitor to the Palace.

He was determined that it would not happen again and he had no intention of Attila ever meeting such a man.

The difficulty was that he was not certain whether the Queen was still scheming for a marriage between him and Attila.

It was an issue he would need to face eventually and he would then put his foot down so there would be no further argument about it.

At the same time he was wondering if he felt well enough for a battle of that kind.

In the following days the Queen made one or two rather vague remarks, but they made him think that she was still in contact with Prince Otto.

'I will wait until Attila returns,' the King resolved, 'then make it very clear once and for all that he is barred from Valdina.'

He could not help thinking that the Queen would be most annoyed and undoubtedly make an unpleasant scene.

'I will wait until I am feeling a little stronger,' the King finally decided.

But he was aware that day was not far off.

The Queen now came into his bedroom looking, he thought, very attractive and she was indisputably a pretty woman.

It was only that her brain and her personality did not equal her looks.

She settled herself down on the side of the King's bed and took his hand in hers.

"I am sure you are better, dearest," she said, "but do not be worried by the Affairs of State as I told the Prime Minister when he asked if he could see you."

"Why was I not told?" enquired the King sharply.

"*I* was told and I indicated that I did not want them disturbing *you*! You are still far too ill to be bothered over matters they can easily settle among themselves."

The King was becoming angry.

"You should have told me that the Prime Minister wished to see me," he said sternly.

"Now do not worry, my dearest. I have settled the whole matter myself. In fact the Prime Minister was very surprised I knew so much about the subject, but he had to admit that my solution to the problem, which was not a big one anyway, was very sensible and something they could put in hand immediately."

The King's lips tightened.

The Queen had no right to give any orders where political matters were concerned and he was most surprised at the Prime Minister accepting them.

At the same time it made it very clear to him what would happen in the future if he was not there to prevent it.

"All you have to do, dearest," she continued," is to get well quickly. Then you can worry about all these little matters, which I do find a tiresome bore!"

The way she was speaking made the King think she was lying and he was aware that she knew she had made a mistake in mentioning the Prime Minister.

Now she was trying to make light of it, hoping he would forget what she had said.

The Queen looked at the clock.

"I am going to undress and then I will come to say goodnight to you and make sure you have everything you require."

She glanced towards the sleeping draught as she spoke and the King wondered why she was so determined he should take it.

It suddenly struck him that perhaps she wanted to look at the State papers that had been left in his bedroom earlier by one of the equerries.

He had not demanded to see the State papers for some time and it did not surprise him that as he had not done so it was known to the Queen.

He was beginning to realise that she had a finger in every pie and a detailed knowledge of everything that went on in the Palace and sooner or later she would undoubtedly turn it all to her advantage.

The Queen rose to kiss him gently on the cheek.

"I will be back in about half-an-hour," she said. "I am sure Frederik is now waiting to attend you."

She walked to the door and turned to wave her hand with a pretty gesture before she left.

As the door closed the King was frowning as every instinct in his body told him she was up to something, but he was not quite certain what it was.

Frederik came in followed by two footmen bringing the Salem water for his bath.

Recently he had found it more enjoyable to take his bath late at night rather than before dinner.

He liked to believe that the cold water was taking away the growth in his chest and he could lie in his bath as long as he wanted to.

Now he thought it rather annoying that the Queen was coming to say goodnight to him and he might not be able to stay in his bath as long as he usually did.

With a strong feeling of resentment he told himself she could wait and he would lie in his bath just as long as he wanted!

The water would undoubtedly help to cure him as Father Jozsef had said it would.

The water had a sweet scent about it and he liked to think of it coming fresh from the beautiful little lake which stood in the centre of Salem.

The people who lived round the lake looked upon it almost with reverence and one of the men who had brought the water to the Palace had told Frederik that it had magic powers.

Another believed that the fish in the lake were the souls of those who had lived in Salem and when they died they could not bear to leave their beautiful village, so they came back in the bodies of fish.

"It's an odd tale, Your Majesty," Frederik had said. "I always says some people believe anything, but it does seem strange that all them that live in Salem be so well."

"Is it really true they live to be over a hundred?"

"I hear as there is one man who be one hundred and five next birthday," answered Frederik, "and a dozen or so be just having their hundredth!"

"It seems incredible," remarked the King, "and we are very lucky that it borders on us."

"Your Majesty can say that again. Someone was saying that when one of the countries up North hears about Salem, they thinks as they'd have a magic lake to attract visitors and just what happened?"

"What did happen?"

"They makes a great hullabaloo about it and when the people came to see it two boys were drowned!"

"That was not very magical, Frederik."

"That's what those people said so they gave up the idea and who could blame them."

"Who indeed."

The King lay in his bath for longer than he would have done otherwise as he was so annoyed with the Queen.

Frederik had dried him and he climbed into bed.

"Your Majesty be later than usual."

"Yes, and Her Majesty is coming to say goodnight to me so you had better leave the Salem water on the chest until she has left. I think it irritates her that I am drinking so much of it, because she said it would do me no good!"

"Your Majesty be proving her wrong. Women be all the same. They always have to be right!"

"So you find that too, Frederik!"

"All of my life I've had some woman whether it be my mother, my sister or one I fancied telling me they were right and I be wrong!"

The King laughed as Frederik was always amusing.

He drank a little Salem water and then Frederik put the glass back on the chest of drawers.

"Suppose Your Majesty wants some in the night?"

"I know I am getting well because I resent everyone mollycoddling me," smiled the King.

"That be more like Your Majesty's old self. When Your Majesty tells I to get out of the way, I know you be well on the mend."

Frederik blew out the lights except the one standing on the table beside the bed.

"Goodnight, Your Majesty," he said, "and may God bless you which I knows he be a-doing."

*

The King smiled as he lay back against his pillows.

He did feel much better and he was determined that tomorrow he would get up and at least sit in the window while he had his luncheon.

He would like to see some of his horses and so he would send Frederik with a message to the stables for his best stallions to be paraded through the garden.

He knew it would please the grooms and everyone in the Palace and the City too would think that if the King was taking an interest in his horses, he would soon be back in the saddle.

'I cannot be grateful enough to Father Jozsef,' the King pondered.

Then he felt as if Father Jozsef was standing beside

him and telling him that he must close his eyes and pretend to be asleep when the Queen came to visit him.

The same old arguments at this particular moment might put him back a pace or two.

As far as he was concerned he had received the message from Father Jozsef and he did not wish to talk to the Queen.

It was only a few minutes later when he heard the door open and he closed his eyes.

He was very conscious that she had closed the door quietly behind her and then she came slowly towards the bed and stood looking down at him for quite some minutes.

The King made certain that his breath was deep and he was positive he looked convincingly asleep.

He was sure that the Queen would think it a shame to wake him and leave the room.

To his surprise she moved to the chest of drawers and he wondered why.

Perhaps it was to examine the water she so disliked him drinking and then he felt there was nothing she could do about it and she would not be so foolish as to throw it away.

Because he was curious he very slightly opened one eye and now he could see that her back was towards him.

She was doing something to the tray Frederik had left on the chest.

'What *can* she be doing?' he wondered.

She was there quite a long time.

The King's curiosity became greater than his desire not to have to talk to her, so he deliberately stirred.

"Oh, are you there, Margit?" he called out. "I must have fallen asleep."

The Queen started.

He thought she almost jumped and it seemed that the mere fact of him speaking had given her a shock.

She came quickly back to the bed.

"I did not want to wake you, dearest," she said.

"I had only just dozed off. I was a little late having my bath and I think you are later than I expected."

"I had some matters to see to before I went to bed and now, dearest, you must go to sleep. I am sure after a good night you will feel better tomorrow."

"I do hope so."

The Queen bent over to kiss him and then she gave a little cry.

"How could your valet be so careless? He has not given you the sleeping draught."

"Oh! I thought I had drunk it."

"No, it is here on the chest of drawers. I will tell Frederik in the morning he is to look after you better. You know what the doctors said."

"I remember it well," the King replied ruefully.

She put the tray with the water from Salem down beside the King with the sleeping draught in a small glass.

The Queen picked up something which was lying in the corner of the tray, but he could not see what it was.

It looked to him to be quite a small object which was entirely hidden once it was in her hand.

The Queen bent forward to kiss him again.

"Now take your medicine and go to sleep. I may have interesting and exciting news to tell you tomorrow."

She did not wait for the King to reply, but walked towards the door.

"Goodnight, dearest. I am convinced that you are getting better, so do not forget your medicine."

The Queen waved to him and left the room.

The King sat up and looked at the tray she had set down beside him.

She had certainly not touched the water.

Yet he was certain the small glass which contained the sleeping draught was fuller than it had been on other nights.

He stared at it for some moments and then he rang the bell for Frederik.

He arrived in a few moments.

"Your Majesty requires me?"

"Close the door Frederik."

The valet came forward a little apprehensively.

"What be going on?" he asked.

"You forgot to throw away my sleeping draught."

"I know, Your Majesty. I think of it after I'd gone. But as you had taken so long in the bath and expected Her Majesty, I forgot to empty it."

"You did not empty it and I have a feeling it is now fuller than when you left."

Frederik bent his head to look at the glass.

"That be true, Your Majesty, there's nearly half as much in again as what I put in while you be having a bath."

There was silence before the King said,

"I want you to take this glass to Doctor Iccus. Ask him to diagnose it and bring it back to me immediately."

Doctor Iccus was a very old scientist, who had been a close friend of the King's father. When the doctor had grown older he had been given rooms in one wing of the Palace.

Doctor Iccus had a charming personality and many of the young students who were interested in science and the development of scientific medicine visited him.

The King knew he was someone he could trust and he would not make a mistake as someone less experienced might do.

Frederik left the room with the glass in his hand.

The King realised he would be away for some time, but now he had no wish to sleep.

He picked up the book he was reading, but found it difficult to concentrate.

What he was thinking was something he could not push out of his mind and yet he had to know if what he suspected was true.

Nearly an hour passed before Frederik returned and when he came forward the King knew before he spoke that his suspicions were not unfounded.

"You woke Dr. Iccus?"

"He was already awake, Your Majesty, and I wait while he tests what were in this here glass."

"And what did he find?"

There was a silence as Frederik drew in his breath.

"It contains, Dr Iccus said, Your Majesty, enough poison to kill a horse!"

The King nodded.

It was just what he had suspected.

He knew now what the Queen held in her hand was the poison Doctor Iccus had given her a few weeks ago.

It had been meant for a very old dog, who had gone blind and on the King's instructions had been put to sleep.

The King thought he knew now what he might have deduced earlier.

The Queen intended to sit on his throne at his death and nothing and nobody was going to prevent her taking what should be Attila's place.

The King sat up in bed.

"Go and waken the Lord Chamberlain," he ordered, "and tell him to come here at once."

Frederik placed the glass down on the chest and left the room.

The King reckoned it would take him some time to reach the Lord Chamberlain and for him to rise and dress.

To his surprise ten minutes later, Frederik opened the door and the Lord Chamberlain entered.

"I received Your Majesty's message as I returned home from a Regimental Dinner," he said. "Can anything be wrong? I was afraid when Frederik asked me to come to you, Sire, you were feeling worse."

"What I am feeling is anger and I am afraid I have a rather unpleasant task for you."

"What is that?" asked the Lord Chamberlain.

"I want you to arrange an Army Escort to take the Queen to her own country and make it plain that if she ever attempts to return to Valdina, she will be brought to trial for attempting to murder me!"

The Lord Chamberlain stared at the King.

He could hardly believe what he was hearing.

"What are you saying, Sire? I can hardly believe what Your Majesty says is true."

"The proof is right there on the chest of drawers. She thought I was fast asleep and added a substance to the sleeping draught I am supposed to drink at night. It has been analysed by Doctor Iccus, who says there is enough poison in it to kill a horse."

He paused and then continued,

"I am not a horse and if I had taken it, as the Queen begged me to do, I should undoubtedly at this moment be *dead*."

The Lord Chamberlain gave a loud exclamation of horror.

"Can this really be true?" he asked again.

"I noticed when the Queen had left, there was more in the glass than previously and Frederik confirmed it."

The Lord Chamberlain gave a deep sigh.

"I will carry out Your Majesty's instructions to the full."

"I apologise for them being so very unpleasant. At the same time we do not need any scandal and the papers must not get to hear of it."

He paused before he added,

"I have, in fact, just thought of a better idea."

"What is that?" the Lord Chamberlain enquired.

"Just over the border into the Queen's country there is the Convent of the Blessed Virgin Mary. You will tell Her Majesty that I will announce she has retired there as it is where she wishes to spend the rest of her life."

His face was grim as he went on,

"That is the message which will go out to Valdina tomorrow and if Her Majesty agrees to go quietly without any protestation, no one except you, Frederik and myself will know the truth."

"I think it is an excellent idea, Your Majesty. The last thing we want at the moment is a scandal of a woman, whether she is a Queen or anyone else, attempting to obtain the throne by such a villainous and appalling action!"

"I leave it in your capable hands. If you wake the Queen now, tell her you can arrange for her to go quietly without a Royal Escort to the Convent, otherwise she will go by *force*."

The Lord Chamberlain gave another deep sigh.

"I am so deeply sorry, Your Majesty, that this has

occurred, but I will carry out your instructions to the letter. I only hope that they will be accepted in a sensible manner and remain a secret to the world outside."

"Thank you, Lord Chamberlain."

The King lent back against his pillows and the Lord Chamberlain thought that the horror of what had occurred was extremely bad for him.

"Please take good care of His Majesty, Frederik," the Lord Chamberlain urged him.

"That's what I intends to do, my Lord."

Now the Lord Chamberlain, none too hurriedly, and feeling extremely apprehensive, knocked on the door of the Queen's bedroom.

CHAPTER SEVEN

There was a knock on Attila's window.

She opened the door to find Lamos outside.

"I've brought hot water, but the gentleman says you are not to hurry as he's gone swimming in the river."

Attila smiled.

She thought it was just like Gesa to take advantage of the nearby river and so she did not dress herself until she heard him return on the other side of the wooden wall.

She wanted to see him and be with him as they had been last night.

Lamos had laid their breakfast out in the same place where they had eaten dinner and as Attila walked over she saw Gesa come round the corner of the carriage.

She waited for him and when he reached her it was impossible to do anything but gaze into each others' eyes.

"You are even lovelier," he sighed, "than you were last night."

Attila slipped her hands into his and she could not find any words which would pass her lips.

They sat down and Kilkos came hurrying over with their breakfast that Lamos had cooked for them.

Attila did not want to eat, but she made an effort to do so feeling that this, like everything that had happened, was something she really wanted to remember and savour in every detail.

Gesa did not speak but kept looking at her.

"Are we going riding?" she asked.

"It is what I would like to do, Lala, but at the same time I think it is more important for us to settle with your family when our marriage can take place."

The way he spoke made Attila feel as if her heart was turning a dozen somersaults.

Then the myriad difficulties and problems waiting ahead for them seemed to rise up in front of her like a huge black cloud.

"Must we go so soon?" she asked him pleadingly.

"You know that I want to stay here forever and you know I want to be by your side for always. How could I want anything else? But as we are both aware there are sure to be obstacles ahead and the sooner we face them the better."

Attila wondered what *his* difficulties would be.

She felt they could not compare with hers.

She wondered desperately whether it would be best to tell him now what was waiting for her at the Palace.

Or should she let him find out for himself when he met her father?

She could not risk losing these last few moments of happiness with Gesa and it would mean bringing up such a controversial subject that they could both be torn apart by it.

"I will do whatsoever you want," she told him in a low voice. "At the same time it is *so* lovely and beautiful here."

She looked out over the grassland as she spoke and a large flock of birds rose into the sky, which she knew the peasants would think a good omen.

She prayed that was what it would be for her.

"Nothing could be more beautiful than you," Gesa was saying. "I still find it hard to believe you are real."

Attila turned her face to look at him.

"I want to kiss you!" he exclaimed. "God knows I want to kiss you again as I did last night. But I think we must settle this matter of our marriage at once because I cannot wait for you without feeling I am going mad!"

'I must tell him that there will be great difficulties ahead for us,' Attila said to herself.

But she could not find the words.

Gesa pushed aside his plate.

"Come, I am feeling like you. As I can read your thoughts, I know that we both have to face the music. We will face it together and I will tell you one thing that under no circumstance will I give you up. You are mine, you are part of me and I have no wish to go on living without you."

He said the words firmly and distinctly, almost as if he was not only addressing Attila but a large audience.

Then before she could even move, he turned and walked away, whistling, as he did so, for Zeus.

The stallion came trotting up to him and Attila went back to the carriage.

Lamos had the horses between the shafts and she walked to his side and said to him in a low voice,

"Listen to me, Lamos!"

"I am listening," he answered.

"We are going back now to Valdina and I want you to take us to Father Jozsef's house. I am intending to leave Mr. Gesa with you there while I go and see my father."

She glanced back to see if he was approaching.

"Mr. Gesa has no idea who I am and, of course, as I have instructed you before, you are not to tell him."

"I'll keep my mouth shut and so will Kilkos."

"I shall not be away for long, but he is not to know where I have gone. I have to see His Majesty alone."

"I understand," said Lamos. "Leave the gentleman to us. We make him comfortable."

"Thank you, Lamos. I knew you would help me."

Attila whistled for Samson who came galloping to her at once. She felt he knew he was going home, back to his own stable, and was looking forward to it.

Lamos saddled and bridled him and Attila collected a few items she had left inside the carriage.

When she went back to Samson, Gesa was already mounted on Zeus who was behaving rather obstreperously.

Lamos helped Attila onto the saddle, hurried back to the carriage and climbed up on to the box.

As Attila joined Gesa, their horses both broke into a gallop and they rode off together over the grassland leaving the carriage moving slowly along the river bank.

They had gone quite far before the horses changed to a trot.

Then Gesa said,

"Has that blown away the cobwebs?"

"I felt as if we were galloping to the very end of the world," answered Attila.

"That is just what I intend to do with you," he said. "When we are married we are going to explore very many places which will fascinate us both. As you know what I do with you will be more thrilling and more exciting than anything I have ever done before in my life."

"How can you be so sure of that?" asked Attila.

"I think you know the answer. We are already one person as we have been before in many, many lives and I knew when I left you last night that we will be married in no more than two or three days!"

Attila gave a little cry.

"No one could be married as quickly as that!"

"Except us! You will find out, my lovely one, that when I want something desperately as I want you, I always get my own way."

"That is just what I want you to have," murmured Attila.

But she was frightened.

They turned back towards the carriage, which was only a dot in the distance, but it did not take them long to reach it.

Now Attila could see the first towers and spires of the City of Valdina and as they journeyed on there were one or two peasants' cottages.

The mountains on the other side of the river were very familiar – she had climbed them all with her father.

As they drove nearer still to the Palace, there was the high peak she could see from her bedroom and which had always been a symbol of inspiration to her.

When she had been a little girl her mother had said,

"You must always strive in life to reach the top of mountains and not be content with sitting at the bottom."

At the time she could not quite understand what her mother meant.

As she grew older she realised that, as Father Jozsef had once said, she must raise her eyes to the stars.

"If you seek the best in life," he told her, "then you must look up towards the sky. For that is where we believe Heaven to be and which gives us the inspiration we need because we live on earth."

She thought now of all the things she had desired, some of which she had already attained.

What she wanted now was not only more important but greater and so high that it was almost out of her reach.

Gesa had spoken very little since they had turned their horses towards Valdina and she thought that perhaps he was praying, as she was, that everything would turn out for the best and that they really could marry each other as they both desired.

She looked up at the peak of the mountain.

'Am I asking too much?' she sighed from her heart.

Then as she prayed the sunshine seemed to glitter for a moment on the peak.

She felt it was an answer to the one question which seemed to consume her.

It took them little less than two more hours to reach the outskirts of the City.

Lamos turned his horses towards the little valley in which Father Jozsef's small house was situated.

When it first came into sight with the spire of the Chapel rising above it, Gesa spoke after what had seemed a long silence.

"Is that your house?" he enquired.

Attila shook her head.

"No, it belongs to Father Jozsef who, as you know, died when I was at the Shrine."

"Why are we going there?"

Attila felt herself trembling because what lay ahead was going to be so very difficult.

"I want you to stay in Father Jozsef's house, while I go first to speak to my father."

"Do you live nearby?"

"Just a short distance which will not take me long," replied Attila.

She swallowed and went on,

"I want first to tell Papa that Father Jozsef had died and second how kind you have been in bringing me home. It might have been much more difficult if I had been alone with the servants."

She thought what she was saying sounded sensible and it would be difficult for Gesa to refute it.

She sensed that he was debating whether he would insist on accompanying her to her father.

Then he said,

"Very well, my darling, if that is what you want to do. But do not be long and if you disappear back into the Heaven from which you have just come, you can be quite certain I will follow you!"

"I am certainly not going to disappear. I want to be with you. Oh, Gesa I love you, you know that. But – there may be – difficulties."

She stumbled over the last few words and Gesa said almost fiercely,

"Whatever they are and however impossible they may seem, we *will* surmount them."

He paused for a moment before he continued,

"We also have the real answer to anyone who tries to prevent our marriage."

"What is that?" asked Attila.

"It is quite simple. We love each other and it is a love which is unconquerable and irresistible. No one shall take it from us."

Attila put out her hand towards him.

"That is just what I feel and what I too believe. Oh,

Gesa, I am praying to Father Jozsef and to God to help us."

Gesa reached out and touched her hand.

The horses were too far apart for him to kiss her as she longed for him to do.

They rode on and a few moments later Lamos drew the carriage up outside the door of Father Jozsef's small, but very attractive house.

Gesa's eyes were twinkling when he looked at it.

"I am sure it is really a doll's house or perhaps a Fairy Palace which will disappear when we touch it!"

"It is very real, Gesa, dear Father Jozsef has given people who call on him such happiness that you will find the atmosphere inside will make you feel that there are no troubles, no difficulties and no danger ahead of us."

"That is just what I wish to believe, my precious one."

They dismounted and left the horses with Kilkos.

Then they walked up the steps to the front door.

Lamos had given Attila the key and she opened it and they went straight into the small sitting room.

It was where Father Jozsef had always welcomed his guests and Attila felt for a moment as if he was waiting for her.

Gesa followed her looking, she thought, rather tall in the low-ceilinged room.

"I can quite understand your Father Jozsef being so happy here. In fact you are quite right, my darling, I can feel all the holiness and peace he gave to so many people in the atmosphere."

"I knew you would understand," Attila murmured.

"Of course I do. Have you not realised by this time that because we belong to each other, our feelings are the same as are our brains."

As he looked back and realised they were alone he put his arms round Attila.

"You are mine, my darling," he asserted fiercely. "*Mine* completely. Whatever troubles may lie ahead of us we are together and we will never lose each other."

Then he was kissing her, kissing her as he had last night.

At first gently then as her body seemed to melt into his, possessively and passionately.

For what seemed an age it was impossible to move.

When at last Gesa raised his head, Attila said,

"Let me go now and see Papa. I will not be long."

"Would it not be easier if I came with you?"

Attila shook her head.

"As I have told you, Papa has been ill and I would not wish him to be upset. I am sure if I tell him my way, it will not be such a shock to him."

Gesa gave a little sigh, but he released her.

"I understand, but please be as quick as you can. I am frightened to let you out of my sight."

"I shall be even more scared in case you have run away while I was gone," said Attila.

"Do you really think that is possible?"

He did not wait for an answer, but pulled her close to him once more.

Almost roughly he kissed her again and again and then he took his arms from her.

"Go now and hurry or else I shall have to come and search for you."

She ran out of the room and hurried through Father Jozsef's garden.

She would have liked to have stopped at the Chapel to say a prayer, but she knew it would delay her.

Gesa might indeed carry out his threat and come to find her!

She ran through the valley and up into the wood.

Then she moved through the trees until she reached the Palace garden as usual ablaze with flowers and blossom and the fountain was throwing jets of water up into the sky.

She did not dally as she usually did to look at the goldfish in the bowl with the water falling down on them like glittering diamonds.

She reached the garden door of the Palace, and as she did so, she noticed an *aide-de-camp* at the end of the passage going into a small sitting room.

She stood very still, hoping he would not see her and then, before he closed the door behind him, he made a Royal bow.

This told Attila to her surprise and delight that her father might be there.

She had thought he would still be in his bedroom and she knew this sitting room was often used by him, but that her stepmother disliked it.

As soon as the *aide-de-camp* had disappeared Attila hurried along the passage.

She paused for a moment outside the door as she wanted to make sure that if her father was there, he was alone.

There was no sound of any talking and after a few moments she opened the door very quietly.

She was right.

Her father was sitting in a large red armchair next to the fireplace which was filled with flowers.

He was reading a newspaper.

Attila ran in closing the door behind her.

The King looked over the top of his newspaper and gave an exclamation.

"*Attila*!"

"I am home, Papa," she cried, running towards him, "but I did not expect to find you here."

She flung her arms round his neck and kissed him.

"I am home, Papa, and it is wonderful to see you."

"I am so thankful you are safely back home, my dearest daughter. Was everything all right?"

Attila gave a little sigh.

"I have very sad news, Papa. When we reached the Shrine, Father Jozsef died."

"*Died*!" the King echoed in surprise.

"We cannot really be sad, because when he died at the Shrine, he loudly called out the name of the woman he had always loved and I know she was waiting for him."

Her father put his arms round her.

"I am sorry, my precious girl, you should have gone through anything so upsetting as Father Jozsef's death."

"He said you would get better, Papa, and you must be as you are out of bed and down here."

"I am much better, but actually this is the first day I have come downstairs, so I must have had a premonition that you would be returning."

Attila slipped to the floor so that her arms were on his knees.

"I have something to tell you, Papa."

"What is it, my dearest?"

"When I was at the Shrine with Father Jozsef," she

began slowly, "I prayed for two things – that you would get well and that I would find love."

"Well, your first prayer has been answered and I knew while you have been away that you were praying for me. I was also conscious once or twice that Father Jozsef was helping me which of course he must have been."

There was a silence and then he asked,

"Who have you fallen in love with?"

Attila drew in her breath.

"You may find this rather hard to believe, Papa, but I know that I have found the man who the Greeks believe is the other half of oneself. I love him so with all my heart and soul just as you loved Mama and Mama loved you."

The King stroked her hair.

"This is just what I have always wanted for you, but you have not yet told me who this lucky man is."

"You may find this even more difficult to believe, Papa, but I do not know his name anymore than he knows mine!"

The King stared at her.

Then Attila told him exactly what had happened.

How Gesa had run to her asking her to save him.

How she had hidden him in Father Jozsef's side of the carriage.

How having shaved off his moustache the man who was trying to kill him had luckily, because it was growing dark, not recognised him.

The King listened without making any comment.

"He has come back with me and he is waiting now in Father Jozsef's house. I said I must tell you first what had happened to me before you meet him."

"That was very sensible of you, my darling, and of course I will see him."

"I love him, Papa, and he loves me. However many difficulties there may be about us marrying, *please*, please because you are so brilliant, think of a solution for me."

The King's hand touched Attila's cheek.

"I love you, my dearest daughter, and you are now all I have in my life."

Attila looked surprised at the way he spoke.

"What do you mean? Has something happened to Stepmama?"

The King hesitated for a moment.

"Because she was determined, if I died, to take your place on the throne of Valdina, I have sent her back to her own land and she will not trouble either of us again."

Attila gave a cry of joy.

"Oh, Papa, I am so glad! Are you certain she will not return?"

"It is impossible for her to do so as she is now in the Convent which as you know is just over the border."

Attila felt there was much more to this story and yet she did not want to bother her father into talking about it until he was ready to do so.

All that mattered was that her Stepmama had gone and she could have her father to herself.

She rose and putting her arms round his neck kissed him on both cheeks.

"What you have just told me, Papa, makes me very happy and now I am going to fetch Gesa to meet you."

"I will be waiting here, my darling."

"I am first going to change my pilgrim's dress."

Attila ran across the room and as she reached the door, she looked back.

"It is wonderful, Papa, to see you downstairs and so

well! That really matters more than anything else."

The King heard her running down the passage.

He was now wondering desperately what he could possibly do about this strange man Attila thought herself to be in love with.

Now he was in better health, he was quite sure he would soon be as strong as he had always been.

The question of his successor was not so important at the moment, but even so when he did die, he still wanted Attila to take his place.

But it would be quite impossible if she was married to someone who was not desirable – a man who would not be accepted by the people of Valdina.

He sat back in his chair speculating frantically what he could do.

How could he break it to Attila that she could not marry the man she loved unless he was acceptable?

The King put his hand to his forehead as if to force his brain into finding a solution for him.

Then he felt that Father Jozsef was near him and he was holding up his right hand in blessing. It was as if he was saying that there was no need for him to worry.

Attila arrived at her bedroom and because she was in a hurry she did not ring for her lady's maid.

Instead she pulled off her pilgrim's dress and put on one of her prettiest gowns, one that her father had once admired and she knew it made her look most glamorous whenever she wore it.

As she was in a hurry she had no time to look at herself in the mirror and any observer would have thought that actually she looked radiant and ethereal.

Her father was well which was something she had not expected and although she had been nervous he had not immediately dismissed the idea of her marrying someone unknown.

She also had a strange feeling for which she could not account – it was that everything since she had returned home was not only better than she expected but perfect.

It was something she could not express in words.

Perhaps it was the serene atmosphere she sensed in Father Jozsef's house that had swept away her misgivings.

The fears that had been with her all night had now disappeared and as she was going back to see Gesa again, she felt as if there were wings on her feet.

She was travelling on the golden rays of sunshine streaming in through the windows.

She ran down the stairs and without stopping by her father's room, she opened the door into the garden.

She ran past the fountain and into the wood.

She thought that the birds were all singing a song of gladness and the rabbits scurrying in the undergrowth were as happy as she was.

'I love him, oh, how I love him,' she told herself, as she ran down into the valley. 'I know Papa is going to love him too.'

Only when she opened the door into Father Jozsef's house, did she feel a moment of anxiety.

Just in case Gesa was not there.

But he was.

When he heard her enter the room, he jumped to his feet.

"You are back!" he exclaimed.

As she ran towards him, he caught her and held her away from him.

"Let me look at you. I have only seen you look like a pilgrim, now you look like a lady."

He gave a little laugh before he corrected himself.

"No, that is wrong, you look like a Goddess or do you prefer to be a Queen?"

Attila made a little sound that might have been one of laughter or surprise.

It was impossible to answer because he was kissing her again.

He was kissing her wildly and demandingly as if he had been afraid that when she left him, she would not come back.

It was a long time before Attila was able to speak.

Then she said,

"Come, Papa is waiting to meet you and my prayers have been answered. He is well and strong again. Oh, I am *so* grateful to the Shrine."

"I think you have another reason to be grateful."

"I prayed for *love*," she whispered in his ear, "and found *you*."

"That is just what I wanted you to tell me," Gesa sighed.

Attila took his hand.

"Come along, we must not keep my Papa waiting. I have a feeling that everything is going to be wonderful and there is no need for either of us to worry."

"I hope you are right, my darling."

They left Father Jozsef's house and walked through his beautiful garden.

"The Father must have worked very hard here."

"I will tell you about it when we have time and I want you to see his Chapel as well."

She was holding his hand and they were moving as quickly as they could up the path through the little valley.

Then they passed through the wood into the garden of the Palace with flowers all around them.

The Palace loomed up beyond the garden wall.

Attila sensed that Gesa was surprised, but she had no wish to make explanations, only to reach her father.

She opened the garden door and Gesa followed her down the passage.

She was half afraid there might be someone with her father.

However, her father's room was quiet as she pulled the door open and he was still sitting in the chair where she had left him.

As she walked towards him followed by Gesa she said,

"I am back, Papa."

The King started as he had not heard her enter and he rose to his feet.

"I want you, Papa, to meet, Gesa, who I have told you about."

The King looked at Gesa and Gesa at the King.

Then Gesa exclaimed in a tone of astonishment,

"Your Majesty!"

Attila's heart gave a lurch.

Then the King called out,

"Prince Gesalo!"

His hand went out as he spoke and Gesa took it.

"You have grown," remarked the King, "if I am not mistaken?"

"No, of course not, Sire, and it is so nice to see you again."

Attila looked from one to the other.

"Are you saying," she asked in a soft voice which

did not sound like her own, "that you know each other?"

The King laughed.

"When I last saw Gesalo he was still a young boy and his father was a friend of mine for many years until he became so ill."

"I am afraid that he is still very much the same, Sire, and now it is only a question of months."

"I am sorry," replied the King. "At the same time I am sure you will agree it will be a merciful release."

"That is what I am prepared to believe."

Attila was still looking bewildered as the King said,

"You told me, Attila, that you did not know who this young man was."

"And I as well did not know who she was, Sire," added Gesa. "I was prepared to abdicate rather than lose her!"

"And I was wondering how I could send you away without breaking my daughter's heart."

They both laughed.

"Is it really true," asked the King, "that your life was in danger and Attila saved you?"

"She saved me when I thought my last moment had come. My cousin, who I do not think you have met, is heir to the throne if I am not around, so was determined to be rid of me. By sheer brilliance your daughter saved me. So you can understand, Sire, why I cannot live without her."

"And I will have to look after him, Papa, in case that horrible man – tries again," suggested Attila.

Her voice was a little unsteady.

She was finding it difficult to believe what had just happened.

How could her father possibly know Gesa?

How could he turn out to be a Prince when she had thought she would not be allowed to marry him?

As if her father sensed her feelings he said,

"Let us start at the beginning, my darling. Gesalo, whose name you said you did not know is the eldest son of His Royal Highness the Prince of Silesia."

Attila gave a little gasp.

She knew only too well that Silesia, on their border to the North, was the largest and richest of all the Austrian provinces.

Silesia had been fought over when Prussia had tried to wrest it from the Hapsburgs and it had, however, gained its independence and the Ruler was of great importance in the region.

She remembered now something her father had said to her some time ago.

"It is said," he revealed, "that the Prince of Silesia has suffered a stroke and is in a coma."

Attila realised that this conversation had been two or three years ago and she had no idea then who would be his successor.

She could now appreciate the vital significance of the Prince's escape from his wicked cousin.

"What I would request of Your Majesty," Gesa was saying, "is your approval for me to marry your daughter as soon as it is possible to do so."

He smiled at Attila.

"I am now fully aware that you are not the humble pilgrim, Miss Lala, but instead the beautiful Princess Attila of Valdina who I have never had the privilege of meeting, but who is constantly being talked about in my country."

"Why ever was I not brave enough to tell you my name?" asked Attila.

The Prince smiled.

"I think it was so confusing for both of us to realise that our love for each other is far greater than anything we could ever possess."

"And I was ready to run away with you if my Papa would not allow me to marry you," murmured Attila.

The King laughed.

"You are not to worry any further. I now give my blessing with the greatest pleasure to the son of my oldest friend. I only make one demand on my dearest daughter."

"What is that?"

"When you produce a son," he replied, "which will certainly prevent your cousin from troubling you any more, I can be his Godfather and you will christen him with my name."

Attila realised he was asking this favour because he had no son himself.

"I think, Papa, that as our two counties are joined to each other, you will be able to help Gesalo – as I must now call him – and he and I will come and help you."

"That is exactly what I would like, otherwise I may be very lonely."

"You will never be lonely, Papa, and if we join our two countries, our children, and I think God will give us a great number, will have two wonderful places to play in."

She could see clearly from the intense expression in her father's eyes how much this meant to him.

"I think, Papa, you must send a very large gift of gratitude to the Shrine of St. Janos. I feel that all this has happened because I went on a pilgrimage to him."

"And I will double whatever you give," the Prince added. "Although I did not pray at the venerable Shrine, I have prayed ever since I met Attila that she would be mine. Now my prayers have been answered."

The King put his hand on Gesalo's shoulder.

"I cannot tell you how happy I am that all this has happened. How soon do you want to be married?"

"Tonight or tomorrow," replied the Prince.

The King laughed.

"That is far too quick. But I do understand with the problems over your cousin and that your father – God bless him – might die at any moment, the marriage should not be delayed."

"That is what we both want."

"And that is what you shall have, Gesalo, and as it is nearly time for luncheon, I will go and give my orders that it must be a very special meal."

He touched his daughter's cheek very tenderly and then he walked across the room and opened the door.

Attila knew he was tactfully leaving them alone for a moment.

It would enable them to recover from the surprise and shock of learning the truth of who they both were and that their positions in life were very different to what either of them expected.

Gesalo put his arm around Attila and drew her close to him.

"Only your father would be so understanding as to let me kiss you. Not as an unknown man, but as a Prince who has gained through the mercy of God the one and only woman in the world to make him happy."

"If you are grateful, I feel the same. I was so afraid that Papa would send you away and that I would have to marry someone like that dreadful Prince Otto."

The Prince made a sound of disgust.

Then he pulled her against him.

"There has never been any question of you being married to anyone but me and just because you are so very beautiful, my darling, I shall be wildly jealous of any man you meet and of any man you speak to!

"After all is said and done I have been searching for thousands of years for you and now I have found you, I am never going to let you out of my sight for a single minute!"

Attila would have replied to his wonderful words of love, but his lips held hers captive.

Now he was kissing her in the same way he had last night.

By this time it was more demanding, because he was so happy that she was his.

Attila felt the same.

She had been so frightened in case he would be sent away and she knew that if that happened her heart would have gone with him and she would never find love again.

'I love you, I adore you,' her whole body was crying out as he kissed her and went on kissing her.

For a moment he raised his head.

"How can you make me feel like this?" he asked. "I adore and worship you. When we are married it will be like Heaven to be living with you."

Then he was kissing her again.

This was Love.

The true love of Father Jozsef, St. Janos and God Himself.

Attila knew their love would increase and multiply as the years went by.

They would never lose each other or the love which had joined them.

Either in this world or in the many worlds to come.